Dear Mystery Reader:

At long last, Biggie is back! Biggie Weatherford—feisty grandmother extraordinaire—turns in a superior sophomore effort in her follow-up performance to the much-lauded BIGGIE AND THE POISONED POLITICIAN.

The debut of this series caused quite a stir both in and outside of the mystery world. Many mystery booksellers had the book high on their recommendation lists, and it was nominated for an Agatha. *People* magazine and *Entertainment Weekly* also gave the book stunning endorsement. Even Bill and Hillary Clinton jumped on the bandwagon, as they reportedly read passages aloud to each other.

So if you're a veteran Biggie reader, I'm sure you've been champing at the bit for Nancy Bell's latest. But if you're still a rookie to Biggie's world, I know you'll want to read on and see what all the buzz is about. Inside you'll find loads of down-home Southern charm, eccentric characters whom you can't get enough of, and Biggie's unfortunate but hilarious run-in with murder. There's never a dull moment when Biggie's around. Enjoy!

Yours in crime,

Joe Veltre

Joe Veltre
St. Martin's DEAD LETTER Paperback Mysteries

Other titles from St. Martin's **Dead Letter Mysteries**

Dead Letter is also proud to present these mystery
classics by Ngaio Marsh

Also by Nancy Bell

Biggie and the Poisoned Politician

BIGGIE
and the MANGLED
MORTICIAN

NANCY BELL

St. Martin's Paperbacks

To Sally Presley, Tom Bell,
Tony and Susan Bell, Rebecca Hughes,
Jim Sewalt, and Jeff Bell

BIGGIE AND THE MANGLED MORTICIAN

Copyright © 1997 by Nancy Bell.

All rights reserved. No part of this book may be used or reproduced in any manner whatsoever without written permission except in the case of brief quotations embodied in critical articles or reviews. For information address St. Martin's Press, 175 Fifth Avenue, New York, N.Y. 10010.

Library of Congress Catalog Card Number: 96-54632

ISBN: 0-312-96491-9

Printed in the United States of America

St. Martin's Press hardcover edition published 1997
St. Martin's Paperbacks edition/March 1998

10 9 8 7 6 5 4 3 2 1

Job's Jottings from Julia

The town is all atwitter over the play being given at the high school cafetorium to help raise money to convert the old depot into a museum. It is an operetta and is called *HMS Pinafore*. It was written by two Englishmen named Mr. Gilbert and Mr. Sullivan. Let's all turn out and make it a rousing success because it is for a good cause.

We had a little excitement in the town square last Tuesday. It seems that Cooter McNutt escaped from the city jail. He would have gotten away but for the quick thinking of Vida Mae Boggs, head shampoo girl at Itha's House of Hair. It was told to this reporter that Vida knocked him to the ground and sat on him until help came. Acting police chief Butch Jenkins stated that he was delayed in apprehending the suspect due to breaking the heel off his boot during the chase.

1

The day Cooter McNutt busted out of jail, I was playing football on the courthouse lawn with Little DeWayne Boggs and his Aunt Vida. Cooter came shooting out of the jailhouse door like a turpentined cat. Butch was right on his tail.

"Stop, you naughty boy," Butch yelled. "You get back here this very minute! You hear?"

Butch is our town florist, but he got appointed deputy police chief after Chief Trotter went to jail for helping Jimmie Sue Jarvis when she murdered the mayor—but that's another story.

Cooter jumped straight up in the air, clicked his heels together, and yelled, "You can't catch me, you faggot. I'm outta here!"

He shouldn't of said that because Aunt Vida, who was getting ready to snap the ball, looked up from between her big fat legs and said, "That ain't a very nice way to go talking to Butch." She stretched out her arm and clothes-lined Cooter just as he ran past her.

"Well, I'll be giggered," Cooter said, scrambling around on the ground trying to get back on his feet. "What'd I run into?"

Butch was getting there as fast as he could, but it wasn't easy because of the uniform he'd ordered out of a mail-order costume catalog. The pants were silver and very tight, and he had on matching cowboy boots with three-inch heels.

"Hold on to him, Vida!" he yelled. "I got my handcuffs right here."

By now, Cooter had got to his feet. Just as he was about to take off running again, Aunt Vida gave him a shove, sending him sprawling in the dirt. Then she did something that made my eyes bug right out of my head. She turned around, hitched up her skirt, and started just kind of easing her body down over Cooter. She gave her rear end a little shake, like a broody hen settling down on her nest, and plopped her big fat self down right on top of old Cooter.

"Ow!" he yelled.

"Just be still," Aunt Vida said. "I ain't puttin' all my weight on you."

Little DeWayne had been trying to twirl the football on the end on his finger like nothing unusual was happening. Now he leaned his pudgy little face over and looked into Cooter's eyes.

"How come you got put in jail?" he wanted to know.

"Get her off me!" Cooter yelled. "I'm gonna smother under here."

Just then, Floyd and Boyd Vanderslice, the twin paper-hangers, strolled over from the domino game that'd been taking place under a big live oak tree next to the courthouse steps.

4

My grandmother, Biggie, says it's a good thing those two are twins because nobody around here would ever get any paper hung if there was just one of them on account of them being Vanderslices. Biggie says all the Vanderslices are so lazy they pray to die young so they can spend the rest of eternity resting in their coffins. She says the two of them together add up to one fair-to-middling paperhanger.

"Whatchall doin'?" Floyd asked.

"They's rasslin', Floyd," Boyd said, "and Miss Vida's got him down for three."

"They're not rasslin'," I said. "Old Cooter's escaped from the jail, and Butch is on his way to take him back. Miss Vida's just holding him 'til Butch gets here."

"You boys reckon you could hold him for a little bit?" Aunt Vida said. "Looks like Butch's broke a heel off his boot."

Sure enough, Butch was sitting down on the curb looking at the bottom of his boot and holding the heel in his hand.

"Me and Floyd can hold him," Boyd said. "Let him up easy, now, Miss Vida. We don't want this here dangerous criminal to get loose. What you in for this time, Cooter?"

Cooter let out a big breath. "Whew! That's better," he said. "They say I chunked a rock through the elementary school window last Saturday night. If I done it, I don't recollect it."

"I know what you mean," Boyd said. "One time I papered over the door to the linen closet in Ida Finchner's bathroom. I didn't even know—"

"He didn't even know he done it," Floyd said. "I told him, I said, 'Boyd, you're paperin' over that woman's linen closet'—"

"Taken us a good two hours extra to fix it," Boyd said.

"We didn't charge her for the extra time, though," Floyd said.

"Wouldn't have been right," Boyd said.

5

Miss Vida rearranged her skirt where it had got all twisted from sitting on Cooter. "Come to think of it," she said, "once I put a red rinse on Vesta Dooley's hair. Well, you know, she prides herself on being a natural blonde. You could of-heard that woman holler three counties away. I don't know how come I done it. I reckon my brain just went for a walk."

By now, a crowd had gathered. Miss Itha came running out of Itha's House of Hair still carrying a comb in her hand, her red hair shining like a brand-new penny. Cooter looked like he'd rather be watching her than eating fried chicken. Biggie and Mrs. Ruby Muckleroy followed close behind. Biggie's hair was wet and sticking to her head; Mrs. Muckleroy's head was covered up with little pink and green rollers. They both had long black bibs tied around their necks that flapped along behind them like Batman's cape. I was sure glad to see Biggie. She always knows what to do in case of emergency.

"J.R.," she said, "you go over there to where Butch is and tell him I said give you his handcuffs. Bring them right back here. You hear? Tell Butch we've got everything under control and he's to go on back to the jail and put some different shoes on."

"Yes'm," I said.

"Well, I *know* everything's under control," Butch said when I told him. "He was under Miss Vida, wasn't he?" He looked at his broken boot and shook his head. "It's broke bad, J.R. I don't know if this boot can be fixed or not. I had um 'specially made, too."

I sat down beside Butch. "What'd you have Cooter in jail for?" I asked. "He says it's because he busted out a window at the school."

"Well, that ain't exactly the whole story, J.R.," Butch said. "Actually, what he did was he busted a window and then

6

stole all the lunch money out of Miss Crews's desk. You know, she collects lunch money for the whole fifth grade, all three sections. We took thirty-six dollars and nineteen cents off of him when we picked him up . . . all in nickels and dimes and quarters. Claimed he needed the money to fix the roof on that old shack he lives in down on the creek bottom."

"Oh," I said. "Well, you'd better give me those handcuffs. Biggie wanted me to get right on back."

"You tell Miss Biggie I'll be waitin' right there in the jailhouse with the cell door open when they bring him back," Butch said, "and that young man's going to bed without his supper tonight. Yesirree Bob!"

When Butch first opened his shop and hung out his red and gold sign that said HICKLEY'S HOUSE OF FLOWERS, Miss Itha got real mad and talked a lot about suing him over the name on account of she said it was plagiarism because her beauty shop had been called Itha's House of Hair for seven years already. That was the main topic of conversation up and down the street for over a month until Mr. Oterwald decided to move his hardware store from the back street to the front street. Guess what he named it. Oterwald's House of Hardware. Well, as you can imagine, that really got Miss Itha's back up. She went to see a lawyer over in Center Point, but he told her she didn't have a leg to stand on because she'd never registered her name at the courthouse. It wasn't long after that that Bertram Handy changed the name of the feed store to Handy's House of Feed.

Miss Itha gave up after that.

"If you're going to live in a town full of crazy people," she said, "you just have to go with the flow."

Mrs. Muckleroy said that wasn't a nice thing to say about Job's Crossing as we had a *few* well-bred people here. She decided to teach Miss Itha a lesson, so she took to driving to Center Point to the beauty parlor. That went on for three whole weeks until that Center Point beautician burned her hair so bad with permanent-wave solution it all fell out and she had to wear a wig for a whole year. After that, she came back to Itha again, but made a point of always mentioning the fact that she's a direct descendant by marriage of James Royce Wooten, the founder of Job's Crossing, and had been elected Grand Worthy Recording Secretary of the Daughters for three years running.

Biggie is president because she is the great, great, great granddaughter of old James Royce.

Me, I'm J.R. I'm twelve years old, and I live with Biggie and Willie Mae and Rosebud in the biggest house in town. Actually, Willie Mae and Rosebud, who is Willie Mae's husband, live in a little house in Biggie's backyard. After Rosebud got out of jail in Morgan City, Louisiana, and came to live with us, Biggie had a room and a front porch built onto the little house. Willie Mae is the best cook in the whole world and a voodoo woman to boot. Rosebud is the best at everything else and has little gold hearts, clubs, diamonds, and spades built right into his four front teeth.

We all went over to the jail and watched while Butch locked Cooter back in his cell. Afterward, Biggie ran her fingers through her wet hair then took off her black bib and gave it to Itha, saying she'd come back tomorrow to finish getting her hair done. After that, Biggie and I started walking back home. We passed Mrs. Mattie Thripp's tearoom just as Mrs. Thripp came out the door carrying a tray covered with a napkin.

"Biggie," she said, "what was all that commotion over at the courthouse?"

"Cooter escaped from the jail," I said. "I helped capture him."

"Is your name Biggie?" Biggie asked.

"No'm."

"Then . . ."

"Yes'm," I said. It don't do to argue with Biggie.

"I doubt if he'll be trying to escape again," Biggie said. "Vida Mae sat on him. By the way, Mattie, I want Norman to play Dick Deadeye in *Pinafore*."

The Daughters are putting on a production of *HMS Pinafore* to raise money so they can convert the old depot into a museum. Biggie is Little Buttercup and I am a British tar in the chorus. Reverend Poteet, the rector at the Episcopal church, is the director and he got Miss Lonie Fulkerson, who teaches piano lessons, to play the music. It's a good thing she can play the piano because she sure couldn't sing. Miss Lonie is as tongue-tied as a hog eating briars.

"I don't know, Biggie," Mrs. Thripp said. "I think Norman had his heart set on the part of the captain of the *Pinafore*."

Miss Mattie sat down on a bench on the sidewalk and put the tray down beside her.

"Rosebud is playing that part," Biggie said.

Mrs. Thripp's mouth formed itself into an O and her eyebrows shot up. "Biggie!" she said. "Who ever heard of a *colored* British sea captain?"

"Rosebud's got the best baritone voice in three counties," Biggie said, "and he's already learned all the songs."

Just then, Mr. Thripp came out the door. He's tall and skinny with shifty gray eyes and thin hair that he grows long and coils around his head like a beanie.

"Mattie," he said, "you'd better get that tray over to the courthouse or Judge Potter's chicken pot pie's going to be colder than a cast-iron commode."

"Guess I'd better," Mrs. Thripp said. "Biggie, I don't guess you'd reconsider?"

"Nope," Biggie said. "It's practically type-casting for Norman to play Deadeye."

"What'd you say, Miss Biggie?" Mr. Thripp said.

Biggie started off down the sidewalk with me following. "Never mind, Norman," she said over her shoulder. "We'll see you at rehearsal next week."

Later, at supper that night, Biggie said, "Norman Thripp had his heart set on singing the part of Captain Corcoran in the operetta."

Rosebud reached out his fork and speared a pork chop off the platter. "Don't make no nevermind to me, Miss Biggie," he said. "I know all the parts. Want me to be Ralph?"

"Rosebud," Biggie said, "that's a tenor part."

Rosebud grinned, showing his gold teeth. "I can sing tenor just as good. I recollect the time I sang 'Mother Machree' on Saint Patrick's day at Paddy's Irish Pub on Bourbon Street. They wasn't a dry eye in the place. Even the Cajuns was weepin' in their Dixie beer."

Willie Mae came in carrying a big coconut cake. "Rosebud," she said, "your tongue gonna keep you out of heaven." She set the cake down in the middle of the table, cut a big slab, and set it right in front of me. "Who *is* playin' Ralph, Miss Biggie?"

"Reverend Poteet," Biggie said. "He's got a fine tenor voice and is good looking to boot. "Meredith Michelle Muckleroy is playing Josephine—if she behaves herself. I declare, that girl's going to drive everybody crazy as bull bats with that silly giggle of hers."

"She can't help it, Biggie," I said. "She's in love with Reverend Poteet."

Biggie snorted. "She's in *something*, all right," she said, "but there's another name for it besides love. Now, J.R., you go upstairs and start getting your lessons. It'll be bedtime before you know it."

"And then you take yourself a good bath," Willie Mae called after me as I climbed the stairs to my room. If Biggie and Willie Mae had their way, I'd spend my whole entire life working or taking baths. The only kid in town that has it worse than me is Little DeWayne. He never gets to play with the other kids unless his Aunt Vida comes along. They're afraid he'll get kidnapped or something. Personally, if I was going to kidnap a kid, it sure wouldn't be Little DeWayne. He can't play ball very good—or do much of anything except help out in his mama's beauty shop. His mama and Aunt Vida make him keep his hair long so they can practice all the latest hairstyles on him. Once he came to school with what his mama called a spiral perm. All the kids in his class called him Corkscrew until his hair grew out again.

They even make him wear a St. Christopher medal around his neck on a silver chain to keep him safe. Miss Vida won it off of one of Mr. Firman Birdsong's Mexican chicken pluckers in a poker game.

2

When I woke the next morning, the sun was shining in my face. My cat, Booger, was sitting on the windowsill watching a nest of baby blue jays outside in the crepe myrtle tree. His tail flicked back and forth like the pendulum on Biggie's grandfather clock. I jumped out of bed and pulled on the jeans I'd worn yesterday and my Houston Rockets T-shirt. It was Saturday, and I had big plans for the day.

When I came down to breakfast, I found Willie Mae standing by the stove making buckwheat cakes which I think taste like grass clippings, but I wouldn't dare tell Willie Mae that.

"Where's Biggie?" I asked.

"Good mornin' to you, too," Willie Mae said. "She be in her room gettin' ready to go back down to that there Hair House to finish up with her shampoo and set. You want one of these hotcakes?"

"Uh-uh," I said.

"Who you sayin' 'uh-uh' to?"

"No, ma'am," I said.

"Want me to fix you a egg?"

"I'm having Fruit Blasters this morning," I said.

I opened the cabinet door and got the cereal down. Willie Mae set a bowl and a spoon on the table.

"You gonna rot out your teeth and stunt your growth," she said.

Just then the screen door slammed and Rosebud came in.

"Oo-eee! Hotcakes," he said. "Sweet thing, you must of been readin' my mind."

"How many you want?" Willie Mae asked.

"Six for starters—then we'll see after that." He rumpled my hair with his hand. "What you plannin' to do today, youngun?"

"Watch cartoons, work on my space-shuttle model, and build a space station in the chinaberry tree out back," I said. "Will you help me with that, Rosebud?"

Rosebud took a big bite of hotcake and washed it down with some of that black Louisiana coffee he likes so well.

"Did I ever tell you about that time I was workin' for them space folks down in Houston?" he asked.

"You worked for NASA? I didn't know that," I said.

"Sure as I was born a Baptist," he said. "Them space guys wouldn't make a move without consultin' me. I was gonna ride up in one of them things, but at the last minute, the feller that runs the mission control room came down with the stomach flu. If I hadn't of taken over his job, they'd of had to abort the mission."

"Gosh!" I said.

"Rosebud," Biggie said from the doorway, "if you'd done all the things you say you've done, you'd be a hundred and thirty years old."

Rosebud just grinned and held out his plate for more hotcakes. "I'll help you this afternoon," he said. "This morning,

I believe I'll just amble on down to the bait shop and see if I can win me a few bucks at dominoes."

Willie Mae was wiping the griddle with a paper towel. She glared at Rosebud. "You ain't goin' to no bait shop," she said. "You're going to stay right here and move the furniture so I can wax the floors." She looked at me. "And you ain't gettin' in my way watchin' cartoons and makin' models. I want everybody out of this house while I'm waxin'."

"You can go with me to the beauty shop," Biggie said. "You can play with Little DeWayne."

That wasn't a totally bad idea. DeWayne has a video game in the back room of the shop called "Raiders of the Planet of Doom," which I'm trying to beat him at. The only thing De-Wayne can do well is video games on account of he plays them all the time because his mama and Aunt Vida won't let him out of the shop that much. DeWayne has already got to level three while I'm still trying to get out of the cave of the saber-toothed android.

"Okay," I said.

We could smell Miss Itha's beauty shop before we even got the door open. It smells good, like shampoo and hair spray and stuff. I heard the ladies talking over the roar of the hair dryer. Itha's House of Hair is a long, narrow building like most of the stores along the square. In back, facing the door, are two black shampoo bowls with chairs to match. Everything else in the whole place is pink and lavender, including the floor tiles and the big dryers and work stations along both the long walls. Butch was giving himself a manicure at the little table near the front door.

Miss Itha was busy putting rollers in Mrs. Muckleroy's hair and Miss Lonie Fulkerson was waiting her turn. Miss Vida was in back shampooing somebody, but I couldn't tell who it was. All I could see was Miss Vida's big behind. She was bending over and you could see the backs of her big white knees spilling over the tops of her hose like Willie Mae's bread dough, and her little bitty feet that looked like they'd break holding up all that weight.

"Come on in, you all," Miss Itha said. "I'll get to you quick as I can, Biggie. I'm busier than a pair of jumper cables at a tent revival. Vernice was supposed to help me, but she came down with a hangover this morning due to being at the dance at the VFW hall until all hours last night."

"Who's that under the dryer?" Biggie wanted to know. She bent down and peered at the person. "Oh, it's Meredith Michelle. What in the world is that all over her head?"

"It's some extralarge rollers," Mrs. Muckleroy said. "As you no doubt know, Meredith Michelle won Miss Job's Crossing last fall and will be going on to the Miss Ark-La-Tex pageant in Texarkana. If she wins there, it's on to Miss Texas in San Antonio!"

"So, what's with the big rollers?" Biggie wanted to know.

"Big hair, honey," Miss Itha said. "You know, you got to have big hair to win in Texas. It's the law or something."

I finally got a word in. "Is DeWayne here?" I asked.

"No, honey. He's at the dentist," Miss Itha said.

"Can I play with his video game?"

"It's broke," Miss Vida said over her shoulder. "He left it out in the middle of the floor, and I stepped on the thing. Busted it clean in two."

"I'm designing her dress," Butch said.

"What?" Biggie said.

"Her dress for the pageant. I'm designing it."

Biggie sat down in the empty dryer chair. "Has she got a talent?" she asked.

Miss Lonie spoke up. "Talent? Honey, that girlth jutht oothing with talent."

"You could have fooled me," Biggie said. "What's she going to do?"

"Well," Mrs. Muckleroy said, "we can't decide between a dramatic reading or a song. She can do both equally well."

"Oh, a dramatic reading," Miss Lonie said. "Much more *cultural*. Don't you think tho, Biggie?"

Biggie shrugged. "I didn't know culture had much to do with it," she said.

"I think she should sing," Butch said, waving his hands around to dry the polish. "Do y'all like this color?" He didn't wait for an answer. "I can design a nice dress for a musical number. Don't know about the dramatic reading. It would depend on what it *was*, don'cha know. I'd hate for her to do that dreadful Scarlett O'Hara 'turnip speech.' No fun making a costume for that!"

"It would be taken from William Faulkner's 'As I Lay Dying,' " Mrs. Muckleroy said. "She'd be wheeled out on stage in a pine coffin. Then she'd sit up, gracefully step onstage to do her reading. Either that, or she'll sing 'I Enjoy Being a Girl.' "

Miss Vida finished shampooing her customer and wrapped a towel over her head. The customer was Miss Julia Lockhart, who writes a column for the newspaper.

"How do y'all like your new preacher?" she asked Biggie.

"Rector," Biggie said, "in our church, we call them rectors. He's awfully young."

"I agree," said Mrs. Muckleroy, "too young for his own good is what I say. A clergyman should have a little age on him."

"Well, I think he'th jutht awfully cute," Miss Lonie said.

"Me too," Butch said.

"At least he's making himself useful directing the operetta," Biggie said. "He's very experienced, you know."

16

"How's that?" Miss Itha asked. "You want some hair spray, honey?" she said to Mrs. Muckleroy.

"Lots," Mrs. Muckleroy said. "I want this hairdo to last a while."

"He wrote, directed, and starred in his class play in seminary," Biggie said. "A musical version of *The Exorcist.*"

"That'th right," Miss Lonie said. "He played the demon because it had all the good lines."

"It got written up in *Anglican Digest*," Biggie said.

Miss Julia was sitting up straight in the shampoo chair rummaging around in her purse. Finally, she said, "Itha Ray, hand me one of them combs and I'll be gettin' the tangles out while I wait. Did y'all hear about Larry Jack?"

"What about Larry Jack?" Biggie asked.

"He's sold the funeral home. He's moving to Houston," she said.

"I'm not surprised that boy is going on to bigger and better things," Butch said. "He could lay out a beautiful corpse. Remember the job he did on poor old Mr. Watson?"

"Ooh, yeth," Miss Lonie said. "Tho thad. Misther Watthon was a good bricklayer, too. I'll never underthand why he hired poor Hoppy Bland to work for him. Everybody knowth Hoppy ain't right bright."

"How'd the accident happen?" Miss Vida asked.

"He was raising a load of bricks up to the roof to make a new chimney for the Hank Furgusons," Biggie said. "They had a pulley up in the oak tree, and Hoppy was supposed to have hitched the rope to a limb but he didn't do that. Instead, he decided to hold onto the rope. It slipped out of his hands and the whole load fell right on Old Man Watson's head."

"Mashed his head right flat," Miss Julia said.

"Anyway," Butch said, "when Larry Jack got through

with him, Mr. Watson looked just like Cary Grant. Now that there's pure-dee artistry."

"Why's he leaving?" Itha wanted to know.

"Business, honey," Miss Julia said. "Larry Jack says there's more business in a day in Houston than you can get in a year here. They're always shooting each other and driving over each other with their cars down there."

"Who's going to take over the funeral home?" Mrs. Muckleroy asked.

"It's a big mystery," Miss Julia said. "All Larry Jack will say is, we'll all be surprised when the new undertaker comes to town. Itha, you'd better look after Meredith Michelle. She's getting mighty red under that dryer."

Miss Vida went and pulled the big hood off Meredith Michelle, who looked like a boiled lobster.

"Can I watch DeWayne's TV?" I asked.

"Sure, honey," Miss Itha said, "you just go on back there."

I watched *Super Heros from Mars* and an old movie, *Flash Gordon and the Mole People*, before Biggie stuck her head around the curtain that separates the back from the front. Her face was all pink and she had little bitty curls all over her head. She sure didn't look like Biggie, who mostly just pulls her hair back in a knot with little curls escaping all around her face. I made a face.

"I went and let Itha talk me into getting a cut and a permanent," she said. "Never mind, it'll grow. Come on, Willie Mae's got lunch ready by now."

While Biggie was paying her bill, I happened to look out the window in time to see a big black car pull into a parking space right in front of the shop and the ugliest man I'd ever seen get out and start toward the beauty shop. He had broad shoulders and long arms and a face that looked like it had been run over by a bulldozer. He came up to the window and shaded his face with both hands and peered into the shop. I guess Miss Itha saw him too because she dropped the pen she was holding and let out a little holler.

"What's wrong, honey?" Biggie asked, turning toward the window.

Miss Itha couldn't say anything, just kept gasping for breath and pointing toward the window. She was white as Mrs. Moody's little poodle, Prissy.

"Help me get her into a chair, J.R.," Biggie said. "Vida! Come here. Something's wrong with Itha."

Before you could say boo to a goose, everyone in the shop was gathered around Itha. Miss Julia told her to put her head between her legs. Mrs. Muckleroy wanted to call the doctor. Miss Lonie said a Dr. Pepper was the best thing in the world for a fainting spell. Biggie said the best thing was for us to all leave so she could relax. Finally, Miss Vida just picked her up in her arms and carried her to the back of the shop and laid her down on the little daybed they keep back there.

"Y'all can go on home now," she said over her shoulder. "I know what to do."

3

In the "Job's Jottings from Julia" column the next Saturday it said, "Job's Crossing has a new undertaker, Mr. Monk Carter, who is fresh out of mortician's school in Fayetteville, Arkansas. He has purchased the Lively Rest Funeral Home from Larry Jack Jackson, who recently moved to Houston. This writer predicts a great improvement in the appearances of our local dearly beloveds as he is sure to know all the latest 'tricks of the trade.' It is not known why our town's most gifted (and only) hairstylist fell over in a dead faint at the sight of him. Is there something you're not telling us, Itha?"

Biggie read it aloud at the breakfast table. "So that feller was our new undertaker," she said.

"Why do you reckon she did that, Biggie?" I asked, "Miss Itha, I mean."

"Who knows?" Biggie said. She was frowning at the newspaper.

Willie Mae set a big platter of something on the table, then scooped a spoonful on my plate. It looked like scrambled eggs—but not quite.

"Eee-yew," I said, "what's that?"

"That there's Hangtown Fry," she said. "Go on, try it."

I poked it with my fork. "I believe I'll just have cereal."

Rosebud picked up the platter and passed it to Biggie, who helped herself to a big serving of the stuff.

"You havin' some, honey?" he asked Willie Mae.

"You know I don't have nothing to do with oysters," Willie Mae said. "You just go right on and finish it up."

Rosebud emptied the platter onto his plate and took a big bite. "Um-um," he said, "I believe I'll have another hot biscuit to finish off with—and some fig preserves."

Biggie passed the preserves, still frowning at Miss Julia's column. "That Julia has been reading Liz Smith again," she said. "Somebody ought to tell her she's no New York gossip columnist. She's going to cause somebody some real misery one of these days." Biggie wadded up the paper and threw it in the trash. She looked out the kitchen window. "It's a beautiful day," she said. "I'll bet the perch out at Wooten's Creek are hungry enough to eat the tail off a dead skunk. I'd give two Sundays in a row to be out there pulling them in."

"Let's go, Biggie," I said.

"Can't, son. Did you forget? I'm giving a garden party tomorrow to kick off the museum's fund drive."

Willie Mae poured fresh coffee in Biggie's cup and handed it to her. "Turn your burners down," she said. "This house is done cleaned up—and Rosebud got the yard lookin' like a golf course."

"Well—" Biggie said.

Before she could finish, me and Rosebud were heading out to the garage to get the fishing poles and tackle ready. We loaded them in the car while Biggie and Willie Mae washed up the dishes. Biggie came out of the house wearing a big red straw hat. She looked like a thumbtack on account of she's not much over four feet tall.

"You drive, Rosebud," she said, "and Willie Mae and I will sit in the back. J.R., you ride up front and hold the poles out the window."

On the way out to Wooten's Creek, we passed Biggie's farm where my friend Monica Sontag lives with her parents. They rent the farm from Biggie for a dollar a year plus all the fresh vegetables we can eat.

"Biggie," I said, "can we stop and ask Monica to go fishing with us?"

"They're not home," Biggie said. "They went over to Commerce to take care of some business."

"What kind of business?"

"Monkey business," Biggie said. "Ernestine Sontag's sister, Doreen, is all upset because that sorry husband of hers lost their farm in a cockfight, but that's not the worst part."

"That's real sad all right," Rosebud said, "puts me in mind of the time Willie Mae's brother lost their daddy's café to Snake Eyes Garcia in a—"

"What was the worst part, Miss Biggie?" Willie Mae asked real quick.

Biggie dug down into her everyday fishing purse and pulled out a comb. "Comb your hair, J.R. You look like Prissy Moody." She turned to face Willie Mae. "The worst part," she said, "was the fact that Doreen's husband was booking bets on those poor old roosters. The sheriff of Hunt County tossed him in jail and threw away the key. Poor Doreen pitched a wall-eyed fit right out in front of the jail, and before they could get her calmed down, she'd broken out with the shingles all up and down her right side."

"I once cured a man of the shingles," Rosebud said. "Doc Thibadeaux over in Natchitoches said it was the worst case he'd ever seen and he just gave up on the poor feller."

"What'd you do, Rosebud?" I asked.

"It wasn't nothing," Rosebud said, "I just went and taken him down to the banks of the Sabine River and rubbed that old black river mud all over him. After that, I made him set in the sun until the clay dried up harder'n a preacher's, uh—heart." Rosebud slapped his knee and laughed without making a sound. "Lord, if he didn't look a sight with skeeters buzzin' all around him and a witch doctor settin' right smack on his nose."

"Why didn't he just brush it off?"

"Well sir, he couldn't of done that on account I'd done told him he couldn't move a hair until that clay dried. I'd told him if one single crack come on his body, we'd have to start right back over at the git-go."

"How come?"

"Trade secret, boy. If I told you, you'd go and tell all your friends and then everybody in Texas would know how to doctor the shingles." He winked at Willie Mae, who was glaring at him from the backseat. "Anyway, after the clay dried, I snuck up behind him and shoved him off the bank into the river. When he come up, all them shingles was gone off his body, and he never had no trouble again. Feller was so grateful, he gimme the best huntin' dog I ever had."

"Whatever happened—"

"Never mind," Biggie said. "Turn here, Rosebud, I want to drive by the Wooten family cemetery and make sure nobody's pushed over any tombstones. I declare, I wish I knew who's been doing that."

"Monica says it's the Wooten Creek monster," I said. "She said she'd seen his tracks all over the place."

Biggie didn't answer.

"Biggie! Didn't you hear what I said?"

"I heard you," Biggie said. "That kind of talk doesn't re-

23

quire an answer, J.R. You know there's no Wooten Creek Monster."

"But Monica—"

"Drive on, Rosebud," Biggie said. "Everything looks— wait a minute. Stop."

Before Rosebud could get the car stopped all the way, Biggie had jumped out and was trotting down the little gravel path that divided the cemetery. The rest of us followed. Biggie stopped in front of her parents' grave and picked up a green vase that had a bunch of dead flowers in it.

"J.R., go over to that hydrant and fill this with water," she said. "I'm going to pick some of those climbing roses and put them on Mama and Papa's grave. I declare, I didn't know they'd still be blooming here in the middle of October."

I started for the hydrant Biggie had had installed for watering the grass but I never made it to fetch that water. What I saw right in the middle of Great-Uncle General William B. Travis Wooten's grave made my blood turn to buttermilk. There in the soft ground was the biggest footprint I'd ever seen in my whole life. Then I saw another . . . and another, leading straight into the woods behind the graveyard. Those footprints must of been bigger than a tennis racquet and a good six feet apart.

As soon as I could get my feet to move, I ran faster than a duck in a hailstorm back to the others. My mouth hadn't quite caught up with my feet, so I just stood there panting and pointing back where I'd come from.

"Well, I'll be switched," Biggie said when she saw the prints.

"Dog my cats!" Rosebud said.

Willie Mae crossed herself then began mumbling spells as she gathered pinecones and arranged them in the shape of a triangle in the middle of the biggest print. Next, she found a smooth gray stone and spit on it before placing it in the center of the triangle.

"We'd best be goin'," she said.

For once, Biggie didn't have a thing to say as we all walked back to the car and climbed in.

The sun was high in the sky when we finally drove down to our favorite fishing spot on the creek.

"How 'bout if we eat now?" Rosebud said. "Them fish ain't gonna be bitin' in this heat."

Biggie thought that was a fine idea, so Rosebud got the hamper out of the trunk and I brought along the ice chest, which held a gallon pickle jar full of sweetened iced tea with mint leaves floating around in it. Willie Mae spread a tablecloth on the ground under a post oak tree and started to unpack the hamper. We had meat-loaf sandwiches made from last night's leftovers and potato salad, bread-and-butter pickles, and deviled eggs.

After we finished, Willie Mae walked into the woods to search for roots and herbs to use in her voodoo spells while Rosebud rolled over and fell asleep.

"Biggie," I said, "was Uncle General William B. Travis a real general?"

"No, son. That was his name, General William B. Travis Wooten. The real William B. Travis was a hero in the Texas Battle for Independence. Uncle met a real general once, though. That Yankee general—Sherman."

"How?"

Biggie sat up straight. The only thing she likes better than fishing is talking about her ancestors. "Well, Uncle General Travis ran a stagecoach inn up in the Oklahoma Territory. Once the general—he was old then—came through traveling west on the stage. Uncle said ne wasn't impressed. By that time Sherman was old and stooped over and had white hair. Uncle General Travis knew Quanah Parker, too. He used to come by the inn every month or so to buy chewing tobacco."

"Who's that?"

"Quanah Parker? He was a great chief—half white. My goodness, J.R., don't they teach you anything in that school?"

"No'm." I decided to change the subject before Biggie decided to educate me herself. "Biggie, where's DeWayne's daddy?"

"What? Oh, well, DeWayne doesn't need a daddy. He's got Vida."

"Biggie—"

Biggie sighed. "J.R., as far as you or anybody else needs to know, DeWayne doesn't have a daddy. My stars! Who taught him to play ball and swim? Who dresses up like Santa Claus every single Christmas—"

"And doesn't even have to wear a pillow." I giggled.

"And who dressed up like a circus clown at his birthday party last year?" she continued.

"I know, Miss Vida."

Biggie smiled. "Right. And who takes him with her every Saturday night when she plays poker out at the Dew Drop Inn? Vida Mae. That's who."

"Biggie, isn't that where he fell out of a tree and broke his collarbone? I don't reckon that's being too good of a daddy. Lettin' him get hurt and all."

"And who walked two miles back to town carrying him in her own arms, Mr. Smarty?" Biggie stood up and put her red hat back on. "Let's walk down to the creek and drown some worms."

I grabbed our poles and followed Biggie down the slope to the creek. Guess what. Somebody had our fishing spot. A funny-looking woman with two kids was sitting on my very favorite rock, fishing. Just as they came in view, the woman pulled her line out of the water with a big old perch just flopping yellow in the sun.

"Well, well," Biggie said. "If it isn't Bettie Jo Darling and her children, Franklin Joe and Angie Jo."

As soon as those two kids heard Biggie's voice, they jumped up and scuttled off into the woods like two possums, their heads poking out in front of them, and their little pale eyes darting from side to side. Their mama looked at the ground, but I thought I saw a smile on her freckled face. The dress she was wearing looked exactly like one Biggie'd worn on Easter Sunday the first year I'd come to live with her in Job's Crossing.

"Biggie, that looks just like . . ." I pointed to the dress.

Biggie didn't answer, just walked over to the woman and got right up in her face. "Catching anything?" she said, real loud.

When the woman answered, I just about jumped out of my skin. Her voice sounded like somebody practicing the tuba when they didn't know how to play very well.

"Doobicle," she said, and held up a stringer full of fish.

"How—are—the—children?" Biggie asked, still looking right in her face and moving her lips real slow.

"Ustgow ime," the woman boomed.

At that moment, Rosebud came bounding down the hill looking like he'd just seen the devil. Biggie gave him a look and he stopped twenty feet away and waited. When the woman saw Rosebud, she ran off in the direction her children had gone.

"Biggie, who was that?" I asked.

"Just someone I know," Biggie said. "Don't be nosy. Let's fish."

"She left her fish. Do you reckon she'll come back for them?"

27

"She'll come back when we're gone," Biggie said. "Rose-bud, bring that minnow bucket out of the car. I feel like catching me a big old bass today."

We fished until sundown and came home with a good catch, which Willie Mae fried for supper. After supper, Biggie said she was going to bed early so she could get ready for her party. I went in and sat on the edge of her bed.

"Biggie, can I ask you just one question?"

"Anything, J.R. You know that."

"Why did that woman at the creek sound the way she did?"

"She's deaf, J.R. She hasn't heard the sound of a human voice since she was three years old and lightning took away her hearing—but none of her wits."

"Well, why did her kids run off like that?"

"You said *one* question, and I answered that. Now, get out of here and let me get my beauty rest."

4

It's raining horse apples and pig knuckles, Miss Biggie. What we gonna do about your party?" Rosebud said as he came in the back door on Sunday morning.

Biggie was sitting at the kitchen table having a cup of coffee and watching as Willie Mae took a pan of little bitty angel biscuits out of the oven. Biggie jumped up and ran to the window.

"God bless America!" she said, and flopped down in her chair.

Willie Mae took a country-cured ham out of the refrigerator and started cutting it in real thin slices.

"Don't worry, Biggie," I said. "You can just call everybody and tell them the party's put off 'til next week."

Biggie looked like she could start bawling her head off any minute. I put my arms around her and looked at Willie Mae. Then I had a brilliant idea.

"Willie Mae can conjure up a spell. Can't you, Willie Mae? Can't you make the rain stop?"

Willie Mae had commenced making little biscuit sandwiches with the ham and putting them on a silver tray just like the party was still going to happen. Finally, she spoke.

"Rosebud, you git in there and start puttin' Miss Biggie's card tables up in the front rooms—and get the good tablecloths out of the buffet. Now, Miss Biggie, you call up that there Butch and tell him we need the altar flowers outta the church just as soon as the service is over."

Biggie stood. "You're right! We'll just have our garden party inside. J.R., put on your raincoat and go outside and pick all the flowers that you see, roses, daylilies, hydrangeas. Spread them out on the back porch to dry. We'll arrange them later."

Before you could say boo to a goose, we had the house all spiffied up and ready for an inside garden party. Besides the little biscuit sandwiches, Willie Mae had made a great huge Lady Baltimore cake and loaded up Biggie's glass tray with strawberries dipped in white and brown chocolate. Butch came in the front door bringing not only the flowers from the church, but two arrangements of bronze mums.

"I was saving these for the homecoming game," he said as he set the mums on the table, "but I reckon I can get some more from Les Fleurs de Henry over in Center Point before Friday night. Now, let's see what we can do with this place."

Butch went to work, and before long the house was a sight for sore eyes. Butch had trumpet vines from Mrs. Moody's back fence spilling out of every corner and wrapped around the stair banister. A big bouquet of yellow daylilies and blue hydrangeas covered the top of the mantel, and the altar flowers, which were white roses, sat right smack in the middle of Biggie's dining room table. Biggie gave Butch a big hug. "I won't forget this," she said. She glanced at her watch. "Holy roller! Look at the time. J.R.,

30

head for the bathtub. Put on that new plaid shirt I ordered from L.L. Bean."

I made tracks up the stairs before she could change her mind and make me put on my Sunday suit.

The party was going great guns when the reverend arrived. Rosebud, dressed in a white coat, was passing trays of food to the people while Miss Lonie sat at the dining table pouring out tea in Biggie's good china cups with the Wooten family crest on the sides. Meredith Michelle, wearing her new blue fall suit with the ruffeldy blouse, kept hanging around the door peeking outside every chance she got. She got a big smile on her face when Reverend Poteet walked in. He had somebody with him—the stranger we'd seen outside Miss Itha's beauty shop.

"Come right on in, Father," Biggie said, taking him by the arm. "Since you're new in town, let me take you around and introduce you to all the folks. Everybody's just dying to meet you."

"Miss Biggie," the reverend said, running his finger around his white plastic collar, "I, er, brought along our new undertaker, Mr. Monk Carter. Knowing your reputation for hospitality and generosity, I just knew it would be all right."

"Of course," Biggie said. "Welcome, Mr. Carter."

The minute Biggie turned loose of his arm to shake hands with Monk, the reverend snuck away and headed for the refreshment table.

Boy, did I get a surprise when that undertaker opened his mouth to talk. He looked mean enough to flush the toilet while you're in the shower, but his voice was smooth as whipped cream on chocolate pudding. He actually *bowed* to Biggie and kissed her hand.

"Madam, your kindness is only exceeded by your beauty," he said.

31

I could of swore Biggie turned pink around the ears.

"Well," she said. "You'll do." She took him by the arm. "Let's get you introduced to a few folks."

I climbed up to the stair landing and watched as Meredith Michelle wiggled her way over to the reverend and grabbed hold of his arm.

After everybody had filled up their plates and gotten some tea, Biggie stood in the middle of the room and rang her little silver dinner bell.

"Everybody!" she said in a loud voice. "Everybody please take a seat. As you know, the purpose of this little get-together is to discuss plans to convert the old depot into an historical museum for our town. We have already raised over half the money through the donkey rodeo, which was held by the FFA boys last June, and the bake sale, for which we have to thank the ladies' society of Saint Thelma's CME Church. Our own Willie Mae Robichaux is president of that organization. Let's give her a big hand."

Everybody clapped and Willie Mae, who was refilling the teapot, ducked her head, aimed for the kitchen, and slammed the door behind her.

Mr. Thripp stood up. "May I have the floor?" he said.

"Is this about your part in the play?" Biggie asked.

"No," said Mr. Thripp.

"Then you may have the floor," Biggie said.

"It's like this," Mr. Thripp said. "Some fellers from out near Hopewell were in the tearoom, and they were saying as how Ma Parker and her gang came through Job's Crossing once back in the thirties—changed trains right at our little depot. These fellers said they had a layover and even ate supper at the old hotel that ain't there any longer."

"I remember hearing about that," Biggie said. "And you think we ought to develop an exhibit on the Parkers in our museum? Great idea, Norman."

The reverend stood up from his chair. "No!" he shouted. then looked down like he wished the floor would swallow him.

"Why in the ever lovin' world not?" Biggie asked.

"Oh, never mind," the reverend said. "I just thought it might not be appropriate. You know, notorious bank-robbing killers and—"

"Wasn't it right after them Parkers robbed the bank in Longview?" Miss Julia said. "I'll look in the paper's morgue and see what I can dig up on it."

"Good, Julia," Biggie said. "Now, let's discuss our final fund-raiser, our town production of *HMS Pinafore*. We still haven't found anyone to sing the part of Sir Joseph Porter. Anybody got any ideas?"

"How about Roy Lee Peoples down at the Eazee Freeze?" Miss Julia suggested. "I've heard he has a right nice voice."

"I don't know," Biggie said. "He can only sing two songs: 'Ghost Riders in the Sky' and 'Mule Train.' "

"He could learn," Butch said. "I know I'd just love to get him out of those old chaps and boots he always wears and into a captain's uniform with brass buttons and gold braid. I'll bet he'd clean up real nice."

Just then that new undertaker, Monk Carter, stood up. "Ma'am," he said in a voice that sounded just exactly like sorghum syrup: sweet and sticky. "Far be it from me to push myself forward, but I once played *The Mikado* in a college production."

"Ooh," Miss Lonie said, "do they put on playth at mortuary thcool?"

"Yes, ma'am. The Little Rock College of Mortuary Science Glee Club was known all over central Arkansas for their excellent musical productions."

Biggie smiled at the undertaker. "Do you have the time for it?" she asked. "Getting your business going and all?"

"Assuming that the populace of this fine city stays healthy—yes," he answered.

"Then that's settled," Biggie said. "Be at Saint Royce in the Fields parish hall at seven o'clock Wednesday night."

Mrs. Moody raised her hand from the back of the room.

"Yes, Essie," Biggie said.

"Well," Mrs. Moody said, "I went to a play over in Delhi—you remember when I had to go stay with Clarice when she had her baby? Well, it was a little theater production of *The Postman Always Rings Twice*, don'cha know."

"I saw the movie," Mrs. Muckleroy said, "the Lana Turner version, back at the old Crystal Theater before it closed."

"Wathn't that where the hardware thtore is now?" Miss Lonie asked.

"I don't think so," Miss Julia said. "Wasn't it next to the Owl Cafe—where Bertha's Boutique is?"

Biggie rang her dinner bell so loud the clapper fell out and rolled under the table.

"Please!" she said. "Now, Essie, what were you saying?"

"So, anyway," Mrs. Moody said like she'd never been interrupted, "they had someone at the door dressed as a postman giving out programs. I just thought that was a nice touch."

"Good idea," Biggie said.

"Just a minute, Biggie," Butch said. "We don't have one single extra *scrap* of a costume for that."

Mr. Plumley from the drugstore spoke up. "Why don't we get Joe Fred, the *real* postman, to do it?"

Before long, everyone was talking at once, and Biggie couldn't get them to stop because she'd lost the clapper out of her bell.

"Dedrick, you ain't got the sense God promised a goose. It don't have to *be* a postman!"

"We could get Vida Mae to dress up in her clown suit."

"Vida don't have her clown suit anymore."

"What went with it?"

"She gave it to the poor."

"She gave a clown suit to the *poor*?"

Biggie disappeared into the kitchen and came back with Willie Mae's gumbo pot and a wooden spoon. She smacked the bottom of the pot with the spoon like it was a Chinese gong. Then she said in a real quiet voice, "Order, please.

"We'll shelve the idea of a costumed program passer," she said. "If no one else has any bright ideas, we'll just close this meeting."

Mr. Oterwald stood up in the back of the room.

"George?" Biggie said.

"My wife, she had a idea," he said, "but I don't know right off how you folks will take to it."

"Spit it out," Biggie said.

"Well, you know that vacant lot out back of the depot?" Everybody nodded.

"Okay," Mr. Oterwald said, "well, some of you might recollect that my mama used to run a boardinghouse on that lot before it burned to the ground in 'fifty-nine."

"Ooh, that wath a good fire," Miss Lonie said. "You could thee it from plumb out of town."

"Didn't last too long, though," Mr. Plumley said. "That old dry wood burned real fast."

Biggie banged on Willie Mae's gumbo pot.

Mrs. Oterwald stood up. "Let me tell it, George," she said, "I declare, you are the slowest thing. Here's the thing, Biggie, me and George are more than willing to donate that lot to the museum committee if y'all'd be willing to put one of them living history farms on it. We seen one of them down in Gonzales. It was just real nice."

"Now, Alma, where the heck do you think we're going to get the money to do that?" Mrs. Muckleroy asked.

"Hush up a minute, and I'll tell you," Mrs. Oterwald said. "My Grandpa Foster's farm has been settin', empty, out near Brushy Creek Bottom for goin' on four years now. Me and Otis thought we could just move the whole thing, outhouse and all, into town and set it up on that lot."

"Sounds like a dandy idea to me," Biggie said. "Let's take a vote. All in favor?"

Everybody in the room raised their hands.

"Done, then," Biggie said. "Dedrick, how about you being a committee of one to talk Mayo Vance into donating his house-moving equipment to do the job?"

"I suppose I could try," Mr. Plumley said.

"I guess that about does it then," Biggie said. "Meeting adjourned."

Since Willie Mae had put away all the food by then, everybody decided to go home.

The rain had brought the first cold snap of the season.

"Let's have a fire," Biggie said. "Is there any dry wood, Rosebud?"

"Miss Biggie, I learnt from a lumberjack up in the north woods to not never let yourself be without firewood," Rosebud said. "I recollect the time . . ."

But Biggie had disappeared into her room to get out of her good clothes. I helped Rosebud build the fire while Willie Mae got supper ready, red beans and rice with spinach salad and hot French bread. We ate on trays in front of the fire.

"Willie Mae," Biggie said, "did you get a look at the new undertaker?"

"I seen him," Willie Mae said, "and that ain't all I seen. I seen a black crow settin' on his right shoulder."

"A crow?" I said. "Willie Mae, there wasn't any crow on Monk Carter's shoulder. I was sitting right smack on the stairs where I could see everything. If there'd been a crow, I sure would have seen him."

Biggie looked at me, and I hushed.

"What does that mean?" she asked Willie Mae.

Willie Mae pulled off a piece of bread and buttered it. "Means death," she said.

"His death?"

"Could be his; could be, he be the cause of death."

"Well, honey," Rosebud said, "he *is* a undertaker."

"That don't have nothing to do with it," Willie Mae said. "And as for that reverend—"

"Biggie," I said. "Why didn't you invite Miss Itha and Miss Vida and Little DeWayne to your party? Isn't Miss Itha doing the hair and makeup for the play?"

"I did invite them, honey," Biggie said. "Itha's taken to her bed, and Vida stayed home to nurse her. Itha was awfully upset after seeing Monk. Oh, my stars, Willie Mae, do you suppose that black crow could have anything to do with Itha?"

"I reckon we'll see soon," Willie Mae said.

5

"Where 'bouts you want your astronaut's seat to be?" Rosebud asked on the following Saturday morning.

I was standing on the ground looking up at Rosebud, who was almost hidden by the big leaves of Biggie's bois d'arc tree. I walked around the ladder and peered up.

"How 'bout if you put it 'way out on the end of that great big limb?" I said.

"You be flyin' for sure if I put it there," he said. "Leastways 'til you hit the ground. What say we put it more closer to the trunk?"

Just at that very moment, Prissy Moody ran out her back door barking her head off at Booger, who wasn't doing a thing but taking a snooze on the fence between our yard and Mrs. Moody's. Now, if Booger had realized it wasn't anybody but Prissy barking, he wouldn't have bothered to move. But I guess he must of been dreaming about that pit bull down the street because he took off like a shot for the

bois d'arc and climbed up the ladder until he got to Rosebud's legs, then he climbed up them.

"Great Falls, Montana!" Rosebud yelled as he teetered on
top of the ladder before crashing to the ground with the ladder on top of him.

I raced for the house faster than a turpentined cat, yelling
for Biggie and Willie Mae. By the time we got back to the
tree, Rosebud was sitting on the ground chunking bois d'arc
apples at Prissy, who was running up and down the fence
trying to find the hole she'd come in through. Blood trickled
down the side of Rosebud's head and splattered bright red
patterns on his white T-shirt.

"Git outta here, you little flea trap," he yelled at Prissy.

Willie Mae took one look and headed out back to her little house while Biggie squatted beside Rosebud to get a look
at his wound.

"Go in the house and get a clean dish towel," she said to
me. "Put some cold water on it."

When I got back with the towel, Willie Mae was patting
something that looked like red clay on Rosebud's head. "We
gotta get him in the house and put some ice on this," she
said. "Can you stand up, honey?"

"My leg hurts," Rosebud said, "but it ain't a bit worse
than the time Justin Tillery drove his tractor over my foot.
Shoot, I chopped cotton for four hours after that. Leave me
alone, woman. I got a space shuttle to build." He stood up.
"Ow! Now I think of it, I might just rest a bit. You got any
iced tea, honey?"

"Well, shoot a bug!" Biggie said when we got Rosebud
settled on the daybed in the den. "I loaned the ice bag to
somebody. Now who was it? Oh, I remember. Mattie needed
it to cool Norman down last summer when he stood in the
sun too long watching the plumbers dig a trench out behind

the tearoom. His old bald head was one big all-over blister." She grinned and shook her head. "Oh, well. J.R., you just get on your bike and go down to Plumley's Drug Store. Tell Dedrick Plumley you want the best ice bag he's got. Just put it on my bill."

"Ow," Rosebud groaned.

"What is it, honey?" That was the only time I'd ever heard Willie Mae call Rosebud "honey" twice in one day.

"I was just thinking how a chocolate milk shake might make my head quit hurtin'," Rosebud said.

"Get him one," Biggie said. "Matter of fact, get us all one. Hurry back, now. You hear? No dawdling on the way."

I wasn't going to dawdle. The thought of that milk shake made me want to hurry on home so I could sit on the porch swing and drink mine real slow so it would last a long time. I would have made it back in no time at all if I hadn't seen something very strange at the Goodwill box on the courthouse square across the street from the drugstore. Two feet were sticking out from the top of the box. I leaned my bike up against the statue of Biggie's ancestor, James Royce Wooten, and went to investigate. I knocked on the metal side of the box.

"Just a minute," a voice said.

"Who's in there?" I hollered.

"Hold your horses," the voice said. "I'm comin' out fast as I can, ain't I?"

Just then, two hands gripped the rim of the box and a head popped up. It was Cooter McNutt.

"Oh, hey, J.R.," he said, throwing a leg over the side. "What you know good?"

"I gotta go to the drugstore," I said and told him about Rosebud. "What you doin' in the Goodwill box, anyway?"

"Lookin' for stuff," he said, "but you won't tell that sissy

40

cop, will you? He might throw me in the pokey again if he found out."

"I gotta go," I said.

Cooter followed me as I climbed back on my bike. "I might just go along with you," he said. "You reckon your Biggie would mind buyin' me a milk shake?"

I remembered how Biggie was always giving stuff away to help the poor so I said I guessed not. While we were sitting at the counter waiting for our milk shakes, Miss Vida walked past on the sidewalk. Cooter sniffed. "Old fat thing," he said. "She ain't nothing like her sister. Ain't Miss Itha the prettiest thing you ever seen?"

I didn't think so, but I nodded. I was just hoping Miss MacLeod would hurry up with those milk shakes. Cooter smelled real bad.

When I got back home, I told Biggie about Cooter.

"Well, you did the right thing," she said. "Cooter doesn't look like he gets two square meals a week. He better not be getting any ideas about Itha, though. That could get him into some real trouble. Now, hurry and drink up. I want you to go with me to the funeral home. I'm taking a copy of the script over to Monk Carter so he can start learning his part."

I swigged down the last of my milk shake fast. "I'm ready right now," I said. "You reckon he's got any dead bodies in there yet?"

"Probably. I heard Old Man Hale passed away in his sleep Thursday night. He used to be station agent at the depot when I was a girl—ran the telegraph office. Many's the night my papa and I used to go down to the depot to meet the ten-thirty from Texarkana. Papa was a cotton merchant, don'cha know. Why, my papa had half this county planted in cotton—"

"Can I see him?"

"Of course not, J.R. You know Papa's dead and buried."

"I mean Old Man Hale."

"J.R., don't be morbid. What do you want to look at an old corpse for?"

I grinned. "I'd rather see the embalming room," I said.

The funeral home is a big white house with tall, round columns. The front porch curves around the side of the house and leads to a door marked PRIVATE ENTRANCE. The front door faces the street. Biggie peered through the oval glass in the center. Someone had put up a little sign next to the door that said ANTIQUES. Biggie read the sign, then twisted a little brass key sticking out from the wall. It made a sound like a telephone.

I shivered like a rabbit just hopped over my grave when I heard heavy footsteps inside the house. Biggie had been to the funeral home probably a hundred times or more on account of, I guess, when you get to be her age your friends are just naturally going to die off on you. But I'm just a kid and it was my very first time. Suddenly, the door swung open and there stood Monk Carter. For a minute he didn't say a thing, just looked at us like a calf staring at a new gate, then stuck out his big, hairy hand.

"Well, come in. Come in. If it's not Miss Biggie and young J.R." As he stood aside for us to come in, his face took on an expression like I'd seen on Deacon Sweeney when he'd pass the collection plate. He folded his hands together and beamed at us. "Has a loved one been called home?"

"Nope," Biggie said. "All our loved ones are alive and kicking. I've brought over your script for *Pinafore*." She pulled the script out of her purse and laid it on a table. "Learn your lines by Wednesday night. That's next rehearsal."

I looked around the room, at the gray walls that looked like granite tombstones, the gray velvet chairs, gray rug, and the big bouquets of silk flowers. I didn't see what I was looking for.

"Where do you keep your dead bodies?" I asked.

"Right over there in the viewing room," Monk answered, pointing across the hall.

"Can I see—" I stopped right there because Biggie had just pinched a plug out of my shoulder. She pulled me over to a pink brocade couch and pushed me down, taking a seat right next to me. Monk perched on the edge of one of the gray chairs like he was hoping he wouldn't have to stay there long. Biggie picked a candy mint out of a cut-glass dish and popped it in her mouth.

"What's with the 'Antiques' sign out front?" she asked.

"Just a hobby of mine," Monk said. "I've always been enamored of fine old things—especially those from the Victorian era. So exuberant, don't you think?"

Monk started in talking about why he appreciated the Eastlake style as opposed to Queen Anne.

"Well," Biggie said, "I just take care of things. I still have my mama's furniture that she bought when Daddy bought the house from Grandpa back in 'twenty-one."

"And as fine a collection of mission oak as I've seen in a long time, Miss Biggie," Monk said. "You have a treasure trove, a veritable treasure trove."

Biggie smiled down at her hands, and I could see we were in for one of Biggie's cozy chats. "I have some things upstairs that belonged to my great-grandmother," she said. "You must come over sometime, and I'll show them to you."

I eased off the couch and walked over to a marble-topped table, pretending to be interested in a bowl of glass fruit. When I saw they weren't paying me any mind, I snuck out into the hall to look around. A dark stairway led to the second floor. Across the hall, I could see light coming from a double door. I tiptoed over and looked into what I figured must be the viewing room. It had a sweet, sticky smell like dead flowers and something else I couldn't name. Over by the windows, I saw what I was looking for: Old Man Hale. I peered into the coffin and when I did, I decided that Monk Carter wasn't half the undertaker Larry Jack had been. I remembered how nice the mayor had looked when he was laid out, smiling even. This old man's face was gray with little pink spots of rouge on each cheek. He had red lipstick on, and his hands were not even clasped across his chest. They were just curled like claws and kind of hanging there out of the sleeves of his old blue suit. I looked at him for a long time, then signed the guest book and went back into the parlor to start fidgeting so Biggie would decide to leave. Finally, she did.

"What on earth were you doing, J.R.?" Biggie asked as she backed the car right through the funeral home verbena bed, knocking over a birdbath. "What was that? Oh, well."

Biggie is known around Job's Crossing as not being the best driver in the world.

"Just looking at stuff," I said.

"What stuff?"

"Old Man Hale."

"J.R.!"

I didn't bother to tell Biggie about what a bad undertaker Monk was. I figured she'd find out soon enough from her friends.

6

Most everybody in town must be here tonight," Rosebud said. "They ain't even a place to park."

It was Wednesday night, and we were on our way to the first rehearsal for *Pinafore*.

"Park over there by that statue of Saint Francis," Biggie said. "That way, we can beat the traffic going home."

"Miss Biggie, I ain't drivin' on no church grass."

"Of course not, Rosebud," Biggie said. "Drive on the sidewalk. Hurry up. We're late!"

Rosebud eased the car up the curb and parked where Biggie had told him to, but I could see by the way the back of his neck got all stiff that he wasn't too happy about it.

Sure enough, the parish hall was full.

"I declare," Biggie said under her breath, "the people in this town are as curious as possums at a picnic."

She hurried up the steps to the stage.

"Everybody!" she hollered.

Nobody stopped talking.

"Attention, please!" Biggie said, louder.

The folks in front turned and looked at Biggie; the ones in back kept right on talking to each other.

Rosebud stuck two fingers in his mouth and let out a whistle loud enough to rattle the rafters. That did the trick, and Biggie commenced talking.

"Now," she said, "I want all the cast members in front. The rest of you sit down in back where you'll be out of the way." She held up her script and called the roll. Captain Corcoran, Rosebud, come up here and stand by me."

The crowd all clapped as Rosebud hopped up on the stage, all except Mr. Thripp, who was biting his thumbnail.

"Next, we'll have Josephine. Meredith Michelle, where are you?"

Meredith Michelle was over in a corner whispering in the reverend's ear and didn't hear until her mother walked over and pinched her on the arm. "Ouch!" she said. "What'd you go and do that for? Oh." She blushed as she walked to the stage.

Biggie continued. "Ralph Rackstraw. Father, I believe that's you. Dick Deadeye. Ah, yes. Norman, come on up."

Mrs. Mattie gave him a push, and he came onstage with the others.

"Let's see," Biggie said. "I'm Little Buttercup, and I'm here, so the only major character left is Sir Joseph Porter, Monk Carter." She stood on tiptoe and looked over the crowd. "Anybody seen Monk?"

Nobody had, so she called for the chorus, which were all the British tars and the sisters and cousins and aunts, to come onstage. It took a while to sort them all out on account of several of the women had to play sailors, because there weren't enough men in the cast. Butch kept saying he didn't know why he didn't get to play one of the aunts since he was making costumes for the whole production. He finally calmed down when Biggie told him he could have extra gold braid on his jacket and wear a wig.

"Now—" Biggie said.

"Biggie!" Mrs. Muckleroy called out, "it says right here on page nine, 'I snap my fingers at the foeman's taunts,' and we're suppposed to sing 'and so do his sisters and his cousins and his aunts.' Now, Biggie, everybody in the world knows taunts doesn't rhyme with aunts. This thing is poorly written, if you ask me—and what the heck is a foeman, anyway?"

Biggie said something I couldn't hear, and Mrs. Muckleroy shut her mouth with a snap.

Mr. Thripp sidled over to Biggie holding his script. "Miss Biggie," he said, "what's my motivation?"

Biggie sighed. "Norman, your motivation is that you're a mean, sorry, ugly so-and-so," she said. "Now, get over there with the others. Where the heck is Monk? J.R., you go find him."

I looked all through the parish hall and outside where some of the men were standing around smoking, but he wasn't there.

"Okay," Biggie said when I told her. "Lonie, you get to the piano and y'all practice the songs while we go look for Monk."

"Drive over to the funeral home," she told Rosebud, when we were in the car again. "Maybe he forgot."

The funeral home was lit up like a carnival when we got there. Biggie walked around to the side entrance and pounded on the door. No one came.

"Monk!" she called. "You in there?"

I put my ear to the door. "I hear water running," I said.

"And I see water running," Rosebud said. "Looky here."

I looked down and, sure enough, water was running under the door.

Biggie stood looking at the water for a minute, then she said, "Rosebud, see if you can open a window, then you can climb in and unlock this door."

Rosebud walked around and tried all the windows that opened onto the front porch, but they wouldn't budge.

"I think they be painted shut," he said. "Wait a minute. This un's givin' a little. Oo-wee! It's tight, though."

After a lot of grunting and straining, Rosebud got the window open about ten inches. "Won't budge one more inch," he said.

"I can get through there, Biggie," I said. "It ain't any narrower than Mrs. Moody's garage window, and I've been through there lots of—" I shut up real fast before Biggie could ask me what I'd been doing sneaking into Mrs. Moody's garage. I'd have had to tell her I'd been feeding a family of baby rats.

"Well, try then," she said, "but you be careful—and come right straight here and open this door!"

It took a while, but I finally shinnied through. Even with all the lights on, it was spooky in there. I peeked into the viewing room to see if Mr. Hale was still there. Then I remembered Biggie saying they'd buried him last Sunday. I opened the door to Monk's private apartment and looked in the bathroom, where the water was coming from. Water was running in the tub and overflowing onto the floor. I turned off the tap, then headed for the door to let Biggie and Rosebud in. That's when I got the shock of my life. I was running through what must have Monk's little sitting room when I tripped on something and fell flat on my face. It was Monk, and he didn't move or say anything, even though I'd fallen right on top of him.

"Biggie!" I yelled and threw open the door.

Biggie glared at me. "J.R., I told you to come right straight to the door and let us in," she said. "Why didn't—oh, my stars!"

Monk was sprawled out on his blue carpet with pink roses all over it. He looked like a gorilla lying there, wearing nothing but his undershorts. Black curly hair covered his whole entire body. His eyes stared up at us and kind of bugged out of his face, which was almost as black as Rosebud's, and a line of spit ran from the corner of his mouth and had made a wet spot on the carpet next to his head.

Rosebud knelt down and put two fingers on the side of Monk's neck for a minute, then looked up at Biggie.

"Dead as a skint skunk," he said. "We'd best call the laws."

"Rosebud," Biggie said, "the only law we have at this time is Butch. I expect Monk died of natural causes, but just in case he didn't, I'd like to have a look around before Butch has a chance to ruin any clues we might find."

"Miss Biggie, you see murder in everything," Rosebud said. "This feller most likely had a heart attack."

"Hmm . . . probably," Biggie said. "Let's see what kind of medicine he took." She headed for the bathroom. "Rosebud, you check out Monk's bedroom."

"What shall I do, Biggie?" I asked.

"Oh, I don't know—come in here with me and check the clothes hamper," she said.

I was heading for the old-timey wicker clothes hamper when I tripped again. This time it was an iron doorstop made to look like an old-timey soldier. I stooped to pick it up, but Rosebud grabbed my arm.

"Use this," he said, handing me a towel.

"This might be a valuable clue," I said kind of loud, hoping Biggie would hear. But she didn't. She was busy pulling bottles and razor blades and stuff out of the medicine cabinet and piling them in the lavatory, mumbling to herself. I wrapped the soldier in the towel and laid it back on the floor.

"This razor looks like he's shaved a cat with it," Biggie said, "and look at this toothbrush. It must be ten years old. What an unkempt person he was. Ah-ha! Prescription bottles!" She raised her voice. "Rosebud, what is Dilantin? Do you know?"

"Dilantin," he said. "Yes'm, seems to me like that's what they give folks that has them fits, don'cha know."

"Fits? You mean epilepsy?"

Rosebud walked back into the sitting room and squatted down, peering at Monk's face.

"Yes'm, I believe that's what you call it. Puts me in mind of Eddie Guidry—feller I used to know. Old Eddie'd have um whenever he seen flashing lights, and when he did, he looked quite a bit like this feller—all black in the face and drooling all over himself. Got so bad, even a traffic light would set him off." Rosebud laughed and slapped his knee.

Biggie put her hands on her hips. "It's not funny, Rosebud. The man was sick," she said.

Rosebud stood up. "Yes'm, I reckon," he said. "Well, anyway, old Eddie went to the doctor and the doctor gave him some of this here Dilantin, and it stopped them fits right off the bat. Almost cost the man a brilliant career."

Biggie started back toward the bathroom, then sighed and turned back to Rosebud.

"What are you talking about, Rosebud? How could stopping his seizures cost him his career?"

"Well, it's like this," Rosebud said. "One day, old Eddie ran out of money and couldn't get his pills refilled. He might have been okay 'til payday if he hadn't of decided to go down to Jackson Square on Saturday night and try to win a few bucks at craps. The minute he got down there

50

amongst all them lights and signs, he fell out on the sidewalk with a ring-tailed tooter of a fit — jerking around — eyes rolling back in his head—"

"Did he die?" I asked.

"Not on your life, boy," Rosebud said. "Like I'm tellin' you, that there was the start of his brand-new career. Feller from one of them fundamentalist voodoo churches came by and figured out that old Eddie was in some kind of trance."

Biggie had gone back to looking through the medicine cabinet, trying to ignore Rosebud. It didn't work.

"Rosebud," she said, coming back into the room, "what in the everlovin' world is a *fundamentalist* voodoo church?"

Rosebud grinned. "Oh, yes'm," he said. "Well, they're the ones that believes everything they reads in a chicken's entrails is the Inspired Word of God. Well, so anyway, they taken old Eddie and made a high priest outta him. Now, every time they need any prophesyin' done, they just shine a flashlight in his face and Eddie falls out on the floor mumblin' and groanin', and the congregation commences dancin' all around him and beatin' on their drums. Then his wife, Gro Mamba Sally, has a vision and interprets all the mumbles and groans. Last I heard of him, he'd done bought him a bunch of new white suits and a big old Cad—"

"Well," Biggie said, "that most likely explains it. Monk must have had a major seizure that caused his heart to stop." She started putting all the stuff back into the medicine cabinet. "Rosebud, call the church and get Butch over here. Tell him not to say what it's about, or we'll have the whole town coming with him. He can call Doc Hooper to come and write out the death certificate."

While Rosebud called, I showed Biggie the iron soldier I'd found.

"It's probably nothing," she said. "Still, it was on the floor, you say?"

"Yes'm."

"Put it in the car, then," she said. "Just in case."

I put the soldier in the car, then sat on the porch to wait for Butch. I didn't want to ever go back inside that place. After a while I heard the siren as Butch's police car rounded the corner of Linden Street. I walked out to meet him as he screeched to a stop in front of the house. Someone else got out of the car on the opposite side. It was Reverend Poteet. Butch had his little silver gun drawn.

"Put that away," Biggie said from the front porch. "We've got a dead man in here, that's all."

"Ooh," Butch said. "Do I have to look at him? I saw a dead person once—before he'd been fixed up and laid out. It gave me nightmares!"

The reverend headed straight for the living quarters and, by the time I got back in, was kneeling beside Monk and fooling with the body. Butch went into the hall to call Doc Hooper.

"Well," Biggie said, picking up her purse, "I guess we've done all we can here. Did you dismiss the rehearsal, Father?"

"Yes, ma'am," he said. "I told them you'd be in touch with a new rehearsal date."

"Good," Biggie said. "We'll be going then. Oh, by the way, Father, how long have you known Monk Carter?"

"Only since he moved into the funeral home," the reverend said real fast. Never set eyes on him before. Not my kind of folks, if you get my meaning."

"Relax, Father. I was just asking," Biggie said.

When we got home, I unwrapped the soldier. "This might be an important clue," I said.

"It might, if he'd had any marks on him," Biggie said. "A thing like that would leave bruises, J.R."

"Oh," I said.

"Don't look so sad," Biggie said. "Monk probably died of natural causes anyway."

I went into the kitchen to tell Willie Mae about Monk.

"Poor little feller," she said. "Set down and let me cut you a piece of this pie. Want some cold milk?"

"Yes'm," I said. "Willie Mae, you're a voodoo woman."

Willie Mae set a big piece of blackberry pie in front of me. "Tell me something I don't already know," she said.

"Well, do you believe everything you read in a chicken's entrails is the Inspired Word of God?"

"Who's been tellin' you that?" she asked, glaring at Rosebud, who had just sat down at the kitchen table.

"Now, honey," Rosebud said, "I was just tellin' um about Eddie Guidry. Remember him?"

Willie Mae let out a sigh. "I swanny," she said. "This child ain't been through enough, findin' a dead man and all, you got to go fillin' up his head with stuff about chicken entrails."

"But do you?" I asked.

Willie Mae patted me on the head. "No, honey," she said. "I belongs to the reformed voodoos. We believe everybody can interpret chicken entrails in their own way. Now, you eat that pie and drink that milk so you can get on up to bed."

7

"Hidy, Coye," Biggie called from the back porch. "Whatchall doing in town so early in the day?"

It was Mr. Sontag and his daughter, Monica, who live out on Biggie's family farm. Monica is my best friend even though she is a girl and only has hair on one side of her head due to being left too close to the fire when she was a baby.

Mr. Sontag opened the tailgate of the truck and drug out a bushel basket. "Brought you the last of the peas," he said. "Purple hulls. Mama's put up peas until all her Mason jars are used up—and the freezer's full. Reckon you can use these?"

"Mighty right, Coye," Biggie said. "You know how I love a good mess of peas and cornbread. Come on in and have some coffee, why don't you."

"Shore," Mr. Sontag said.

Monica stood on tiptoe and whispered in his ear, and he nodded and went back to the truck. The next thing I knew he'd pulled the biggest pumpkin I'd ever seen out of the bed of that truck. It must of been as big around as a washtub.

"I raised it myself," Monica said. "Look, it's got your initials growing in it. See? Right here near the stem. J.R.W. See? I scratched it on there with a knife when this pumpkin was just a little bitty thing."

I had to smile. That Monica is always thinking of something dopey like that. I guess it comes from living 'way out in the country with nothing much else to do.

"Can we make a jack-o'-lantern out of it, Biggie?" I asked.

"Sure, honey," Biggie said. "It's probably too pithy to eat, being so big and all."

"How come you're not in school?" Monica asked as we sat on the back steps eating Willie Mae's chocolate chip cookies.

"Teacher work day," I said. "How come you're not?"

" 'Cause I'm here bringing you a pumpkin," she said. "Anyway, I didn't want to go to school today. It's boring."

"You're lucky," I said.

Monica picked a blade of Johnsongrass and started waving it along the ground in front of Booger. Booger got real crazy and commenced leaping around trying to catch it. "Not lucky," she said, "just smart. Heck, I make all A's whether I go or not. Mama taught me to read before I was three."

"You'll have to go every day next year when you're in junior high and have to ride the bus into town," I said, "or Mr. Finley, the principal, will come looking for you."

"Yeah, maybe," she said. "What are you doing on Halloween?"

"Going to the school carnival," I said. "What are you gonna do?"

"Be bored," she said. "They're having a party at our church, but it's just for little kids."

55

I had an idea. "Why don't we ask if you can spend the night with us on Halloween?" I said. "Then you can go with me to the carnival."

Monica's face lit up like a jack-o'-lantern. "Yeah," she said. "What shall we wear?"

"I might go as a dead person," I said. "I've seen two of those lately—and they're really scary."

"Good," she said. "I'll be one, too. Hey! Why don't I go as a dead person that's been scalped by Indians. We could smear fake blood and stuff all over my bald spot!"

"Sounds good," I said. "Maybe we could have a tomahawk sticking out of your head."

We were still talking about our costumes when Mr. Sontag came out of the house and said it was time to go. He told Monica she could stay here for Halloween if Miss Biggie didn't care. Biggie said she didn't, so it was settled.

Just as the Sontags drove off, Willie Mae came out of her house wearing a white dress, white stockings and gloves, and a big white straw hat. "What you starin' at, boy?" she said. She didn't even wait for me to answer, just turned to Biggie. "Miss Biggie, if you don't mind, Rosebud's gonna carry me over to the church in the car."

"Not a bit," Biggie said. "J.R. and I will just walk to the tearoom."

"Oh, no, Biggie," I said. "I got plans!"

"Well, if you have plans to eat lunch, you'd better come with me," Biggie said. "Willie Mae has her deaconesses' meeting and doesn't have time to cook. Anyway, Mattie's having chicken-fried steak today, and that's your favorite." She waved her hands at me like she was shooing a cat. "Go on, now. Comb your hair."

Miss Mattie's tearoom is the sissiest place I've ever been in. There are ruffles on the windows and on the chairs and

56

even on the apron tied around Mr. Thripp's skinny old waist.

" 'Morning, Norman," Biggie said as we walked in. "Are the others here yet?"

"They are seated in the azalea room," he said. "Come this way." He picked up two menus and started to lead us toward the back, but Biggie was way ahead of him and had already taken a seat beside Miss Lonie Fulkerson before he could even pull her chair out.

Most of the Daughters were there. Mrs. Muckleroy was telling Miss Julia about Meredith Michelle's dress for the pageant, blue with silver beads. Miss Crews was telling Miss Lonie she'd finally found a store in Tyler that could fit her in shoes.

"You know, I wear a ten quad," she said. "Used to have to order all my shoes from a place in Chicago. Well, this store just had the lovliest selection." She giggled. "They sell to transdresstites, and some of them have really big feet."

Biggie had been in the middle of spreading her napkin in her lap. She looked at Miss Crews. "They sell to who?" she said.

"Transdresstites." Miss Crews lowered her voice. "You know, those men that like to dress up like women."

"Oh," Biggie said.

"I thaw one of them on Ricki Lake latht week," Miss Lonie said. "He wath real pretty."

"Biggie," Mrs. Muckleroy said, "did I tell you Meredith Michelle's had her colors done?"

"What?" said Biggie.

"Her colors," Mrs. Muckleroy said. "I took her over to this woman in Center Point that does your colors for only ten bucks. Meredith Michelle's a perfect Spring—and Bunny, that's the woman's name, said that's real rare. She said only

57

about fifteen percent of the women in the whole world are Springs. The majority are Summers and Autumns. That's why Meredith Michelle's going to look so splendid in that blue dress I bought her."

"Essie, you need to get back on your nerve medicine," Biggie said. "Now, does anyone have any ideas for the museum?"

"I do," said Miss Julia Lockhart. "I think we should capitalize on the Ma Parker visit." She dug down into her purse and pulled out an old newspaper clipping with a picture attached. "I found this in the newspaper morgue."

I stared at the picture while Biggie read what the words said.

JULY 8, 1935

Doyce Hale, station agent for the Cotton Belt Railroad, reported that about noon on Tuesday, when the 11:05 from Waco finally rolled into town, who should step off the train but the famous "Ma" Parker and her boys. Doyce said he was scared at first but that they were just as nice and polite as anyone and asked where was a good place to have lunch. When he sent them to the hotel, they tipped him a whole dollar. Doyce stated that they stayed around back of the depot not bothering anybody for a good hour before their train pulled in, and they left. Doyce stated further that "Ma" was wearing a navy blue straw hat with a red hatband.

"I remember that," Miss Lonie said. "It was jutht the talk of the town!"

"That hat?" Miss Mattie asked.

"No. The event, thilly," Miss Lonie said.

"Lonie, you were only three," Biggie said.

"I thtill remember," Miss Lonie said. "Momma alwath thaid I was thmart as a whip."

"I wasn't even a gleam in my daddy's eye in 'thirty-five,'" Mrs. Muckleroy said.

"We might be able to use this in the museum," Biggie said, "although it's not much. Too bad they didn't rob the bank while they were here. Oh, well. Get that clipping copied and enlarged, will you, Julia? We can frame it and maybe get some old pictures to go with it."

"There's more," Miss Julia said, handing Biggie another clipping. "This one's got a picture."

I looked over Biggie's shoulder while she examined the picture.

"My land," she said, "this one feller looks familiar, but I can't quite figure out who he looks like."

"Let me see," Mrs. Muckleroy said. "Hmm, Ma Parker and her two boys, Rocky and Buck. It says here they got clean away after robbing the bank in Longview." She held the picture out as long as her arm would reach. "I declare, that one on the left looks a little like Reverend Poteet—only meaner."

"Essie, you need to get you some glasses," Miss Mattie said. "Anybody want dessert? I've got some real good pecan pie."

"Not us," Biggie said. "We've got to go."

"Biggie!" Miss Julia wailed, "you haven't even told us about finding Monk last night."

"Nothing to tell," Biggie said. "He was lying on the floor, dead as an anvil. So far, it looks like natural causes."

"I found him," I said.

"Ooo, you poor little thing," Miss Mattie said. She reached to pat me on the head, but I ducked in time.

"Come on, J.R.," Biggie said. She was already standing

with her purse in her hand. "Fine lunch, Mattie, but the quiche was a little runny."

"I know," Miss Mattie said. "Norman just hasn't got the hang of fine gourmet cooking yet. He's coming along, though."

I wasn't surprised. Mr. Thripp had never intended to wind up cooking in a tearoom. He used to be city manager of our town before the mayor went and got himself killed. Mayor Gribbons was Mr. Thripp's only friend and had hired him for the job. The first thing the city council did after the mayor died was to fire Mr. Thripp on the grounds that he'd steal the fillings out of your teeth while you were eating corn on the cob. Biggie said after that, he had no choice but to marry Miss Mattie, who'd been waiting upwards of ten years for him to pop the question. Biggie said he'd probably never find another job on account of who else but Osbert Gribbons would hire a jug-eared, bald-headed crook with all the charm of a scalded water moccasin.

The sky was cloudy, and the wind had kicked up when we came out of the tearoom.

"Step lively," Biggie said. "Looks like we're in for a blue norther."

"Biggie, look," I said, pointing across the square at three people walking into the wind, their heads sticking out in front, like possums.

"Well, I'll be switched," Biggie said, "if it's not Betty Jo Darling and her two kids. What in Sam Hill is she doing in town?"

Just then Betty Jo stopped in front of Itha's House of Hair. Cupping her hands around her face, she bent over and looked in the window. The two kids did the same thing, and they all three stood peering into the beauty shop like people watching a peep shoe in an arcade. Pretty soon, the curtains

60

drew together real fast and I could see Miss Vida's big hand as she propped the CLOSED sign against the glass.

"I declare," Biggie said, "what else peculiar's liable to happen in this town?"

"What are you talking about, Biggie?"

"Them. In town," she said. "You tell me, have you ever in your life seen those three in town?"

"I never saw them at all before last Saturday, Biggie. You know that."

"No, I guess you haven't," Biggie said. "Well, let's hurry on home. It's getting colder than a witch's lips out here."

8

That night, after supper, we all sat around the fireplace in Biggie's bedroom drinking hot cocoa. To make conversation, I brought up the subject of the Darling family.

"Where's their daddy, anyway?" I asked.

"He was killed," Biggie said. "You want me to pour you some more cocoa?"

"No'm, but I could use another marshmallow." She handed me the sack, and I dropped three in my cup. "How was he killed?"

"Industrial accident," she said. "Quit eating those marshmallows or you'll gum up your plumbing."

Rosebud grinned. "Yessiree, Bob, it was an industrial accident all right. That there Donny Joe Darling got hisself ground up in the mixing vat out at the brick plant."

"No foolin'," I said. "How'd they get him out?"

"They didn't," Rosebud said. "They just put a bunch of bricks in his coffin and buried that. Wasn't no way they could get him outta that there vat."

"Rosebud!" Willie Mae said. "Stoppin' your tongue's like tryin' to catch a sack full of flies."

Rosebud grinned at her and continued. "You know that new drive-in bank they built over on River Street? Wellsir, they tell that half the bricks in there's got Donny Joe Darling in um. They say he makes up a portion of the new field house over at the high school, too."

"Wow!" I said.

"Fact is," Rosebud continued, "if you look real close, down low on the west wall of the drive-through bank, you'll see his big toe. Gotta study it real close, though."

Biggie drained her cup. "Time for bed," she said.

"Aw," I said, "can I ask just one more question?"

"Make it a short one," Biggie said, "and ask me—not Rosebud."

"Why do you reckon Miz Darling and her kids were spyin' through the window of Miss Vida's place today?" I asked.

"That's an easy one," Biggie said. "I don't know. Now, scoot up to bed. Tomorrow's a school day."

The next day, after school, I rode my bike home by way of River Street so I could examine the new drive-through bank. I examined those bricks one by one all the way up as high as I could see, but not once did I see anything that looked even a little bit like a toe. I got back on my bike and started home, all the time trying to figure out a way to get back at Rosebud for tricking me. When I got to the funeral home, I saw Butch out front tying a yellow bow on the magnolia tree in the front yard. A police car was parked in the driveway.

"What you doin'?" I asked.

"Securin' the crime scene," he said, stepping back to admire the tree. "Don't it look pretty?"

Then I noticed he'd tied another bow on the pomegranate bush and stretched it across the front of the yard. The ribbon had GO FIGHTING TURKEYS printed in gold glitter all the way across.

"Guess so," I said, "but how come you're using this fancy ribbon? And who say's it's a crime scene? Biggie says Monk's dyin' was an accident."

Butch put his hand on his hip. "Well," he said, "Miss Biggie's smart all right, but I don't guess she knows everything. The ranger's here right now, and he says it's prob'ly murder. As for the ribbon, well, I didn't have any—Hey! J.R., where're you goin'?"

I was already halfway down the block, peddling as fast as I could to get home to tell Biggie about the murder.

Butch had just finished blocking off the driveway with his yellow ribbon when Biggie drove right through it and stopped her car behind the black-and-white Texas DPS car.

"Miss Biggeeee!" Butch wailed.

Biggie opened the door and got out. "Oh. I'm sorry, Butch," she said, "but maybe you'd best tie your ribbon to the porch railing so as not to block the drive. How'd you expect this police car to get out?"

Butch took off his policeman's hat and slapped his forehead. "By jingo, you're right," he said. "Well, how will it look if I put a really big bow on this buttress here?"

"Perfect," Biggie said over her shoulder as she opened the door to the private entrance. "Yoo-hoo. Anybody here?"

I followed Biggie into Monk's little private sitting room. The furniture was old like what we'd seen in the public part of the house, but smaller and more, kind of, cozy. The little settee was covered with flowerdy cloth, and a lamp next to it had a shade that reminded me of the stained-glass windows in our church. Sunlight streamed in through the lace curtains on the windows. It wasn't near as scary as the night we found Monk there. Two men were standing by the door leading to the bathroom. They stopped talking when we came in and stared at us for a minute. One of the men was short and stocky and wore a beige uniform. I recognized him because I'd seen him around the courthouse. He was the state trooper assigned to Kemp County. His name tag read JOHN WAYNE ODLE. The other man was tall with kinky red hair and big ears that pointed, like airplane wings, away from his head. The skin on the back of his neck was wrinkled into little squares like alligator hide. I knew right away he was a Texas Ranger because he wore western pants and cowboy boots. The badge on his white shirt was in the shape of a silver Texas star in a circle.

The trooper frowned. "This here's a secured crime scene, ma'am. No one's allowed in here but us officials."

"Oh, you'll be wanting to talk to us, all right," Biggie said. "We found the body last night. Now, what's all this talk about murder?"

The trooper moved like he was about to usher us out the door. "Later, ma'am. Y'all just go on home now. Us laws will be callin' you when we're ready to interrogate you."

Biggie looked at his badge. "Odle," she said. "Are you Nunly Odle's boy from out near Willow Springs? You must be. All the Odles were built right close to the ground. How's your mama and them? Is your daddy still making syrup? Lord, that Nunly sure could cook up a good batch of sorghum syrup."

While the trooper was trying to figure out which question to answer first, Biggie walked over to the ranger and stuck out her hand. "Biggie Weatherford's my name," she said. "What's yours?"

The ranger's blue eyes twinkled as he shook Biggie's hand. "Red Upchurch, ma'am," he said, "and I'm mighty pleased to meet you. Word is, you're mighty handy to have around when a crime's been committed."

I could of sworn Biggie blushed.

The ranger commenced filling Biggie in just like he was talking to another lawman. "At first, we thought just like you did—that that old boy had maybe had a seizure or a heart attack. Doc Hooper said he was prone to epileptic seizures and had come to see him right soon after he moved to town to get his medicine prescribed."

Biggie sat down on the little settee and the ranger took a chair opposite her.

"So what changed your mind?" she asked.

"It was after old Doc Hooper went to poking around on him. He made what you might call a surprising discovery. Turned out every single one of his ribs were busted—busted bad. And his sternum was mashed clear down into his abdominal cavity."

John Wayne Odle had moved over to join Biggie and the ranger. "Yeah," he said, "and there was little red speckles all over his eyeballs. That's a sure sign he'd smothered to death. Yep. I discovered that myself. Didn't I, Red?"

"Sure did, son," the ranger said. "You'll make a lawman yet."

"It was just like a big old grizzly bear come in here and given him a bear hug," John Wayne said.

Biggie went out to her car and came back carrying the iron soldier still wrapped in the towel.

"You'd better check this out for fingerprints," she said. "J.R. found it on the floor behind the clothes hamper."

I was getting bored, so I slipped outside to talk to Butch, who had picked some orange flowers off the pomegranate bush and stuck them into his yellow bows. "Now," he said, "if I just had some bridal wreath to go with this."

"I think there's a bush around back," I said. "I'll go look."

I walked around the house and, sure enough, growing right next to the window to Monk's bedroom was a bridal wreath bush. Only thing was, it was October and there wasn't a single flower left. I decided to pick a few stems anyway, in case Butch wanted to use the green part. Just as I started to pick the first piece, I noticed something lying on the ground. It was an old, worn-out wallet. As I bent down to pick it up, I saw something else, something that made me forget all about bridal wreath and the wallet. Right there, under that window, were two footprints, but not just any old everyday footprints. These footprints were humongous—bigger than any I'd ever seen. Right away I remembered the prints we'd seen on Uncle William B. Travis Wooten's grave—and Willie Mae's reaction to them. I stuffed the wallet in my pocket and hightailed it back into the house to tell Biggie and the ranger that the Wooten Creek monster had been peeking in Monk's window.

"What on earth are you talking about, J.R.?" Biggie said. "A twelve-year-old boy ought not to believe in such foolishness."

"Just come look, Biggie!" I said.

Biggie sighed. "We might as well humor him or he'll never shut up," she told the ranger.

When we got to the spot, I pointed to the footprints.

The ranger squatted down and stared at the ground, then went to his car and came back with a measuring tape. He measured the prints crosswise and up and down. Then he measured how deep they were.

"No human made these prints," he said. "And no animal either, far as I can tell."

Biggie shook her head so hard her little curls bounced up and down. "Well," she said, "there has to be some explanation, because there is *no* Wooten Creek monster. That's just a load of chicken teeth!"

"But Biggie," I said, "look how deep they are. Do you think it could be an elephant?"

"Don't be silly, J.R.," Biggie said. "It rained last night.

Anyone could have made those prints, and the rain off the roof would have washed down and made them bigger." But she looked real puzzled. "Come on, it's time to go home and get washed up for supper."

The ranger shook hands with Biggie. "Mighty nice to meet you, ma'am. I'll give you a call when we get the report back on the doorstop."

That night, I took the wallet out of my pocket and turned it over in my hand. It was an old tooled-leather thing laced together with a black thong. I'd made one just like it at camp last summer. I started to take it to Biggie, then decided to do a little investigating of my own. I sat on the bed and emptied the wallet out on my bedspread. Inside, I found a coupon for ten cents off on a pound of coffee from the Piggly Wiggly, a picture cut out of a newspaper of a grasshopper so big it took four men to hold it—the caption underneath said GIANT GRASSHOPPER FOUND IN NEBRASKA—and an old lottery ticket. I put the stuff back in the wallet and shoved it in my desk drawer, intending to give it to Biggie the next day.

That night I dreamed the Wooten Creek monster had turned into Reverend Poteet and was chasing me all around the square wearing his Sunday vestments and trying to baptize me.

9

"Rosebud, what do you reckon I ought to wear on Halloween?" I asked a few days later.

Rosebud brought up a cooking spoon full of pumpkin goo and dumped it on the newspaper Willie Mae had spread on the front porch.

"Wellsir, you could go as a pirate—or a hobble-goblin."

"Naw," I said, "I want to be something different. Do you reckon Biggie'd let me shave all my hair off? Then I could go as a person that'd been scalped by Indians, like Monica."

Rosebud wasn't listening to me. He was holding that pumpkin over his head and staring inside. "Seems to me like she's about ready," he said. "What kind of a face you want carved on her?"

"Something real scary," I said. "I aim to clabber the blood of every kid that comes here trying to trick-or-treat us," I said. "Let's make a knife sticking out of it and blood running down from the hole. Oh! And let's have blood running out of its eyes and mouth too."

Just then, a shadow fell over the front steps and a voice said, "Hey there, J.R. Hey, Rosebud. Whatchall doin'?"

It was Miss Vida, all dressed up in her blue dress with little white rosebuds all over it and a lace-trimmed collar. She had white shoes on her little tiny feet. They looked like they hurt considerable.

"Hey, Miss Vida," Rosebud said. "You lookin' for Miss Biggie?"

I jumped up and opened the screen door. "Biggie!" I called. "Biggeee!"

"What is it, J.R.?" Biggie said as she came down the hall from the back stairs. "What have I told you about hollering like a horny moose every time you need me? You're supposed to come find me and speak in a civilized voice. Oh—" She'd gotten to the door and seen Miss Vida standing first on one foot, then another.

"Yes, ma'am," Miss Vida said.

"Well, Vida Mae," Biggie said. "Come on in this house and pull those shoes off. You look like you're about to topple over." She raised her voice. "Willie Mae! You got any coffee left over?"

The porch creaked as Miss Vida headed for the front door. "I wouldn't mind," she said, and followed Biggie into the house.

I went along, too, because, as Willie Mae says, I'm as curious as a bucket of cats.

Miss Vida stopped in the dining room and headed for one of Biggie's little rosewood dining chairs but Biggie took her by the arm and steered her toward the kitchen.

"Let's sit in here," she said. "I always say the kitchen's the best place for a good talk."

Miss Vida let out a big breath of air as she flopped down on one of the captain's chairs we use in the kitchen. The expression on her face made me think of Monica's daddy's

70

bull, Orenthal, when he can't get across the fence to visit with the neighbor's heifers.

"You look like you could eat oats out of a churn this morning, Vida," Biggie said. "Something bothering you? Here, take a slug of this coffee. It'll revive you some."

A big tear rolled out of Miss Vida's eye and then stopped on the end of her nose. Finally, it fell off and splashed right into her coffee cup. She didn't even notice, just took a big gulp of coffee. Finally, she spoke. "It's Itha," she said. "She's done went off somewhere—and she's taken my baby boy with her. Miss Biggie, I'm so lonesome, I just don't know what to do—lonesome and scared."

Biggie waited for her to say more but she just took another drink of coffee and wiped her nose on her sleeve.

"Willie Mae," Biggie said, "have we got any more of that applesauce cake you made?"

Willie Mae nodded and lifted the lid off Biggie's cut-glass cake stand. She cut a big slab and put it on a plate for Miss Vida.

"I might take a little of that," I said.

"You ain't spoilin' your lunch with no cake," Willie Mae said. "They be plenty for after."

Miss Vida ate her cake without saying a word, then pushed her plate aside and started in talking.

"Miss Biggie," she said, "you know I ain't never been accused of bein' what you might call bright."

Biggie didn't say anything, just nodded.

"But sometimes I know things. I don't have to figure things out—just *know* um, don'cha know?"

Biggie nodded again. "Second sight," she said.

"Huh?"

"Never mind. Go on," Biggie said.

"Well, last night, while I was watchin' *Mister Ed* on that old-timey channel they got on cable, it come to me."

"What came to you, Miss Vida? What?" I said.

Biggie gave me a look, and I shut up.

"It come to me that something real bad's happened to Itha and my baby. I just know it, Miss Biggie."

Now, the tears started pouring out of her eyes and running down her face. Biggie handed her a napkin.

Willie Mae had been standing by the sink with her arms folded, just looking and listening. Now she took Miss Vida's plate and cut her another piece of cake, then poured more coffee in her cup. Then she went out the back door and I heard the door to her little house bang shut.

Miss Vida took a bite of cake and commenced talking again. "You recollect the night my precious baby, DeWayne, was born?"

"Lord a mercy, Vida. Of course I remember it. I was there, wasn't I? I took her to the hospital."

"Yes'm," Miss Vida said. "Well, do you recollect how Itha wouldn't tell who the baby's daddy was even though them nurses tried the biggest part of the next day to get her to?"

Biggie crossed her arms on the table and sighed, like she'd finally figured out there was not going to be any chance of hurrying Miss Vida up with her story. "I remember," she said.

"Well," Miss Vida said, "that baby's daddy wasn't nobody else but Monk Carter, that there new undertaker that went and got hisself kilt."

"Hmm," Biggie said.

"Yes'm." Miss Vida started in talking real fast. "I suspicioned he was about half mean the first time I laid eyes on him. But do you think Itha'd listen to me? Not on your life, she wouldn't. 'Course, she was only eighteen and spoilt rotten. We'd all spoilt her, Mama and Daddy and me and Big Mama and Big Daddy and—"

"How'd she meet him?" Biggie asked.

Miss Vida picked up her coffee cup, saw it was empty, and put it down again. "Well," she said, "we was still livin' out on the farm with Mama and Daddy. That Monk, he come off down here from Arkansas sellin' Watkin's Products outta the back of his car. At first, he'd only come around once't or twice't a year. Then, I don't know, seemed like ever' time we'd turn around, there he'd be pullin' up in his old car with the Watkin's sign on the side, and Itha'd be runnin' out to meet him and hangin' her head in the window before he could even get out of the car. Pretty soon they was playin' grab-ass. He'd be chasin' her around the yard and grabbin' hold of her so she couldn't move. And she'd be gigglin' and squealin' like a litter of pigs."

"Didn't your parents object?" Biggie asked.

"They was old, Miss Biggie. They just thought it was harmless frolickin'."

"So she finally ran off with him, I guess."

"Yes'm. Wasn't a thing said. One day, he come, and she went, wavin' at us out the car window until that car was plumb outta sight. Miss Biggie, all this talkin's makin' me dryer than a haystack."

Biggie got up and poured some iced tea out of the pitcher Willie Mae'd left on the drain board. Then she plucked a sprig off the mint plant growing in a pot on the windowsill and dropped it in the glass. "Here," she said, setting the glass in front of Miss Vida, "this ought to oil your pipes. Go on."

"Well 'm," Miss Vida said, "I'm kindly hungry, too."

Biggie sighed and cut Miss Vida another piece of cake.

Miss Vida took a big bite and commenced talking again. "We didn't hear from her for pert' near six months. Like I said, Itha Rae was spoilt rotten back then. She just never taken no mind of what others might be feelin'. Then we got this letter from Minden, Louisiana, sayin' they'd bought a little house and she was expectin' a baby in March. No word about when she might be comin' home for a visit or nothin'."

"So was that the last you heard until that night?" Biggie asked.

"What night, Biggie?" I asked.

Biggie looked at me like she'd forgotten I was there. "Oh," she said, "the night I found Itha getting off the bus in front of the drugstore. I'd gone down to fill a prescription for you. Remember when you had the chicken pox? Anyway, I'd just got your lotion and was going to my car when the bus pulled up and who should be getting off but Itha. Big as a barn and with two black eyes and a fat lip. 'Honey, what's happened to you?' I said. And she told me she'd run away from her husband and had come home for good."

"That's right," Miss Vida said. "Miss Biggie taken her straight to the hospital and called me up on the phone. Didn't you, Miss Biggie? And Little DeWayne was born that very night. And Itha wouldn't tell a soul who the daddy was and made me promise not to tell. They finally had to put De-Wayne Boggs down on the birth certificate on account of Itha wouldn't have it any other way. Ain't that right, Miss Biggie?"

"So that's why she had such a hissy fit when she saw him looking in the window that day," Biggie said. "Poor thing. Can't blame her." Biggie got up and poured herself a glass of tea. "So, where'd she run off to, Vida?"

Miss Vida started looking sad again. "That's just it, Miss Biggie," she said. "She left to go spend some time with Aunt Minnie and Uncle J.C. up in Broken Bow, Oklahoma, until she could figure out what to do about Monk, but she never . . . she never . . ."

Biggie nodded her head. "She never got there?"

"That's God's own truth, Miss Biggie. She never even got there. I called up to Aunt Minnie's to find out how they'd made the trip, and Aunt Minnie and them claimed they hadn't never heard from Itha, much less seen her. Miss Biggie, where can she be? And where's she taken my precious baby boy?" Miss Vida let out a howl that would petrify a possum.

"Calm down, Vida," Biggie said. "Just let me think a minute. Did she have any friends in Minden she might have gone to?"

Miss Vida wiped her nose with the back of her hand. "No, ma'am. Not that I know about. The way she always told it to me, old Monk wouldn't let her make no friends. Itha said he was the jealous type."

"Well, hell's bells, Vida!" Biggie said, "she's got to be somewhere. Think!"

Miss Vida started in blubbering again. Biggie handed her a napkin just in time to keep her from wiping her nose on her sleeve. "There ain't no place. That's what I'm tellin' you. Oh, Miss Biggie, what's done happened to my little sister? What's went with my baby?"

Biggie leaned over and patted Miss Vida's hand. "Never mind, sugar," she said. "Biggie'll find out. You just go on home and unruffle your feathers. I'll let you know as soon as I know something."

Miss Vida leaned toward Biggie like she was about to give her a big kiss.

"Get your shoes on, Vida," Biggie said, standing up real fast. "J.R. will walk you to the door."

Miss Vida leaned over with a grunt and started messing with her shoes, then said, "I can't get um back on. I reckon my feet must of swelled."

"Well, you can't walk home barefooted, Vida," Biggie

said. "I know! J.R., go out to the garage and find that box of stuff Mr. Crabtree left here. Bring back his leather bedroom slippers. Lord knows he'll never use them again."

"Aw, Biggie."

"Scoot!" she said.

I scooted, but I wasn't happy about it. I didn't want to think about Mr. Crabtree, or the night me and Monica watched while he got stabbed to death in the dunking booth at the carnival, or about how we both got kidnapped afterward.

Later, after we sent Miss Vida shuffling down the sidewalk in Mr. Crabtree's slippers, Biggie and I sat on the front porch and watched as Rosebud put the finishing touches on my jack-o'-lantern. He'd taken eggshells and pushed them through the eye holes, then painted red lines on them to look like bloodshot eyes. Red paint was running out of every hole.

"That enough blood for you? Or do you think we could use some more coming out of his nose?" Rosebud asked.

I thought it was perfect, the scariest pumpkin I'd ever seen.

"Biggie," I said, "what are you gonna do about Miss Itha? You promised Miss Vida—"

"I know I did, J.R.," she said. "I'm going down to talk to that Texas Ranger first chance I get. He's probably got folks he can contact in Oklahoma. Truth is, I've got a feeling if we can solve Monk's murder, the mystery of Itha will take care of itself. Now go get washed up, both of you. Willie Mae's got a cold lunch all ready in the fridge."

10

Three days later, I pedaled my bike home from school as fast as I could. I had to get home in a hurry on account of me and Biggie were planning to drive out to the farm and pick up Monica, who was spending the night so she could go to the Halloween carnival with us.

When I came in the back door, Willie Mae was sitting at the kitchen table working a crossword puzzle.

"Slam the door, why don'cha?" she said. "Mor'n likely, you've gone and made my cake fall flatter than a ironing board."

I went to the fridge and poured me out a glass of milk. "Oh, boy," I said. "What kind? Can I have a slice when it's ready? I'm so hungry I could eat a horny toad."

Willie Mae peeked in the oven. "Well, it ain't fell," she said, "but you ain't eatin' any of this here cake. It's goin' to the Halloween carnival for the cake walk. Get you some cookies out of the cookie jar."

"What kind is it?" I asked.

77

"Devil's food with coconut frosting," she said. "Four layers."

"I'm gonna win it then," I said.

Willie Mae put her hand over her face to cover up a smile. "Reckon you could try," she said. "Now, go on out back and find Rosebud. He calls himself rakin' up leaves under that bois d'arc tree. He's takin' you to the farm to pick up your little friend girl."

I took a big bite of chocolate chip cookie. "Whersh Giggie?" I asked.

"You be talkin' with your mouth full, how I'm gonna know what you're sayin'?" Willie Mae asked.

I swallowed the last of my milk and gulped down the cookie. "Where's Biggie?"

"Down to the jailhouse talking to that ranger feller," she said. "She walked to town so you and Rosebud could have the car. Now git, or you won't be back in time for supper."

I found Rosebud leaning on his rake and talking to Mrs. Moody over the back fence. "If I was you," he was saying, "I'd pinch them chrysanthemums off at the tops. It'll make um branch out, and you'll get right smart more blooms."

"Rosebud, you're a treasure," Mrs. Moody said. "I tell everybody, I say, that Biggie Weatherford is the luckiest woman alive to have somebody like Rosebud keeping up her yard."

"Yes'm, I reckon you're right about that," Rosebud said. "Well, looky here. My boy's home from school. You ready to head out to the farm, youngun? I got a surprise for you."

"What?"

"You'll see soon enough. Now go get in the car."

When we got to the farm, Monica was sitting on the front porch with her little overnight bag beside her.

"What kept you all?" she said. "I've been waiting here for four hours."

"Some of us have to go to school," I said. "You got your costume in there?"

"You bet! It's one of Mama's old flannel nightgowns. I'm pretending it's a shroud. You know, on account of I'm a dead person."

I didn't know what a shroud was, but I sure wasn't going to let Monica know. "Well, let's go then," I said. "Willie Mae's gonna help us with our makeup after supper."

"Hold your horses," Rosebud said. "I got to have a word with Monica's mama and papa before we head on back."

"Why?" I asked.

"Curiosity kilt the cat," he answered, and stuck his head inside the screen door. "Anybody home?" he called.

Mrs. Sontag yelled for him to come on in, and he disappeared into the house. He was back before a cat could lick his fanny and Mr. Sontag followed, carrying Monica's sleeping bag and her hunting jacket and her hat with the flaps on the side.

"What's that for?" me and Monica said together.

Mrs. Sontag, who reminds me of an apple because she's so round and has red hair and rosy cheeks, came out the door carrying something white in her hand. "Why, Rosebud's gonna take you kids on a camp-out tomorrow night," she said. "Here, honey, stick these in your bag. It's an extra pair of clean underpants."

Monica grabbed them and stuffed them in her bag, not looking at me. "Whoopee!" she said. "Let's go!"

We had cold boiled ham with potato salad made with baby new potatoes with the skins left on and baked beans for supper. Willie Mae was just pulling a pan of hot biscuits out of the oven when we walked into the kitchen. The cake for the cake walk was sitting on the drain board. It looked prettier than a whole litter of bird-dog puppies. Biggie was already sitting at the table drinking a glass of buttermilk.

"Run and wash your hands, you two," Biggie said. "I could eat a scalded water buffalo."

For such a little bitty woman, Biggie sure eats a lot. I've seen her lay away six whole catfish at one time—with coleslaw and hush puppies on the side.

"What'd you find out from that ranger feller?" Rosebud asked Biggie.

"Not much," Biggie said. "He's as puzzled as I am as to how Monk got mashed up like he did."

"Maybe somebody ran over him with a car," Monica said.

"Yeah, that's real smart," I said. "He was in his living room."

Monica threw a biscuit at me. "How was I supposed to know, Mr. Smarty?" she said.

"Here, now!" Willie Mae said.

Biggie spooned another helping of beans on her plate. "Actually, we did think of that," she said, "because of the way he was flattened out like roadkill. It must have taken a huge amount of force to do that to a big man like Monk."

"I know, Biggie," I said. "Maybe somebody dropped one of those heavy coffins on him."

Rosebud spoke up. "Wellsir, if they did that, there'd of had to be about four murderers. Them things is too heavy for one feller to handle."

"Not them cheap ones," Willie Mae said. "They made out of pasteboard. You remember the time they buried poor old Edgie Jackson and it come a rainstorm?"

"Reckon I do," Rosebud said. "That coffin got plumb soaked through, and Edgie fell out the bottom and rolled down the hill into a little lily pond they had there. All the pallbearers took off runnin' and me and the preacher had to get Edgie in the ground."

Biggie shook her head. "I doubt it was a coffin," she said, "but something did it—and I've got an idea that when we find out what it was, we'll have our murderer."

"Couldn't any human do that," Monica said. "I'm bettin' on the Wooten Creek monster. Shoot, I see his tracks all over the place. Once I even caught a glimpse of him runnin' through the woods. Old Buster like to went crazy barking."

"There is no Wooten Creek monster," Biggie said. "Anybody want any more of this potato salad? I believe I'll just finish it off then."

After supper, I said, "Willie Mae, me and Monica will help with the dishes."

Willie Mae looked at me like I'd gone crazy as an outhouse rat. "What'd you say?" she asked.

I picked up mine and Monica's plates and carried them to the sink. "I said we'd be more'n happy to help you clean up the kitchen," I said.

"What you got on your mind, boy?" she asked.

"Well, I was just thinking that, you know, if we helped with the dishes, you'd have more time to help us with our costumes," I said.

"Git on in there and watch TV 'til I gets through here," she said. "Best thing you can do is stay outta my way."

After what seemed like a very long time, Willie Mae called us to come on out to her house to get ready. "Bring y'all's clothes you gonna wear," she said.

Willie Mae's got her little house fixed up real nice. She has a shelf with all her spells and potions in glass bottles lined up on it. Over that hangs a picture of the Virgin Mary. She's got a bunch of candles, all burned down to different sizes, lined up on the mantelpiece. Her silk shawl with the dragon embroidered on it in gold thread, which was given to her by Sister Sylvester, her voodoo teacher, was spread out on the table next to the bed. The kitchen table was cleared off, all except for a little bitty, old-timey suitcase that Willie Mae called a "train case." When she opened it up, we could see that it was all full of little pots and jars and pencils and brushes.

"What's all this, Willie Mae?" I asked, picking up one of the jars.

"Hands to yourself, *if* you don't mind," she said. "It's my makeup kit what I used to use gettin' folks ready for Mardi Gras day." She started poking around in the case. "Y'all sit yourselves down in these chairs while I figure out how we gonna make you scare the gizzards outta them other kids." She put her hand under Monica's chin and tilted her head toward the light. "We'll start with you," she said. "J.R., you go on outside and set on the steps 'til I call you."

It was good dark by then, so I sat and watched some bats catching bugs around the streetlight on the corner. I was trying to figure out how I could catch one of them to scare the girls with when Willie Mae opened the door and Monica came out walking real stiff and holding her hands out in front of her. She looked just like the living dead I saw in an old movie, *Revenge of the Murdered Zombies.* Her hair, what she had left, was all messy and sticking out all over the place, but her bald spot was oozing with red blood and yellow stuff that I figured was supposed to be pus. Little pieces of skin hung down all around it. Her face was grayish white except for around her eyes and her lips. Willie Mae had painted them blacker than a well digger's pocket. Her hands were white, too, hanging out of the sleeves of her mama's nightgown, and had long yellow fingernails.

I couldn't do nothin' but just stare at her until she grinned at me and said, "Your turn."

I hadn't been able to find anything to wear for a costume until Biggie came up with an old black raincoat that had belonged to her last husband, my Grandpa Weatherford, who had driven out of town in 1953 in his old Packard touring car and hadn't been seen since. When I put it on, it was just barely long enough to cover my shoes. Then I buttoned it up under my chin. Monica said I looked just exactly like Uncle Fester in *The Addams Family*.

When Willie Mae got through with me, I looked a good bit like Monica except for her bald spot. Willie Mae found an old gray wig that used to belong to her *grand-mère* and stuck it on my head.

"Ooh-wee, look at you," Monica said. "You like to made my stomach do a tap dance."

I ran to give Willie Mae a hug, but she pushed me away. "Don't you be gettin' that greasepaint all over my clean clothes," she said. "Just get on outta here and scare them other kids from here to next Sunday."

Rosebud was sitting at the kitchen table holding the car keys when we came back to the big house. He glanced at us.

"Y'all ready?" was all he said.

"Well?" Monica said.

Rosebud grinned. "Well, what?"

"Ain't we scary? Ain't you shakin' in your shoes?"

"I reckon you'll scare them other kids," Rosebud said. "It's just that I seen that same makeup on the Hebert twins the time Willie Mae put a hex on Reverend Smalley for refusing to funeralize her Uncle Theodore on account of his widow didn't have twenty bucks to pay for the sermon. When that preacher got a look at them twins, he taken a spell and couldn't speak a word for three and a half years.

Of course that put quite a dent in his revenues on account of he had to go for three full years without preachin' no funerals or conductin' no weddin's—"

"Let's go," I said. "Where's Biggie?"

"In her room gettin' ready," Rosebud said. "She ain't goin' now. Miss Lonie's pickin' her up later."

11

When we got to the gym, Monica was about to run right into the crowd when I caught her by the arm.

"Looky here," I said, and pointed to a sign hanging by the door. It said:

COSTUME CONTEST at 9:00

FIRST PRIZE: A brand-new all-steel tackle box from Oterwald's House of Hardware.

SECOND PRIZE: A shampoo and set from Itha's House of Hair (free conditioner thrown in).

THIRD PRIZE: Dinner for two at the Owl Cafe.

Monica went and peeked in the door at all the people. "Shoot," she said. "We're a cinch to win. Look at all them kids dressed up like pirates and clowns and witches and devils. I don't know about those prizes, though. What do you think, J.R.?"

"Well," I said, "I guess I could use a new tackle box. And I could give the shampoo and set to Biggie, but I sure don't know what I'd do with free dinner at the café. Willie Mae cooks a whole lot better than Arthel Durley, who's cooking down there now."

"Let's enter anyway," Monica said. "It'll be a honor just to show all them other kids up."

The ceiling of the gym was covered with orange and black crepe-paper streamers, and around the walls someone had hung cardboard cutouts of jack-o'-lanterns and black cats. Cardboard skeletons hung down from both basketball goals. Somebody had draped fake cobwebs all over the place.

"Let's walk in real slow," Monica said. "We'll knock 'em dead when they see our costumes."

She was right. When we walked into that gym, everybody just stopped and stared. They backed off and made a circle around us, whispering to each other and trying to figure out who we were. Finally, Regis Lumpkin, dressed in a clown suit, stepped out of the circle and pointed at us.

"I know who it is," he said. "It ain't nobody but J.R. and his friend Monica from out at Miss Biggie's farm. See, she ain't got any hair on one side of her head."

After that, the other kids all gathered around us asking questions about our makeup and stuff. Finally, everybody left but Regis.

"Gosh dern, Regis," I said, "what made you come as a clown? That ain't scary."

"I'm a *mean* clown," he said, and pushed his big red wig back off his forehead. "See? My mama painted my mouth turned down, and my eyebrows are pointing up—like I'm mad. I'm the meanest clown in the whole world."

Monica patted him on the head. "I think you're real mean

looking, Regis. I sure wouldn't want to meet up with you on a dark night."

"Can I hang around with you?" Regis asked. "I just know my mama's goin' to sit at that bingo table all night. She's already told me so. Can I, J.R.? Please?"

I was about to say no on account of Regis being the biggest sissy in town and a tattletale to boot, but Monica spoke up first.

"Sure you can," she said. "What do y'all want to do first?"

All around the sides of the gym were booths that the PTA had set up to make money. They had Go Fishing and a House of Horrors and a Country Store where you could try to ring jars of home-canned fruits and beans and preserves with embroidery hoops. The fifth grade had set up an apple-dunking booth, and down at the end, I could see Meredith Michelle selling caramel apples and popcorn balls at the Daughters' booth. The middle of the gym was reserved for the big bingo table and the cake walk. I sneaked a glance to make sure Willie Mae's cake hadn't been won yet.

Mr. Finley, the principal, was standing on a little stage they had rigged up in front of the bleachers making a speech, which nobody was listening to on account of the sound system wasn't working.

"I got a idea," Regis said, "how come we don't just start at one end and work our way all around the gym? That way, we won't miss nothin'."

Personally, I thought Regis had a lot of nerve, trying to make up the rules after we'd been nice enough to let him hang out with us, but it seemed like a good plan so we started at the fishing booth. Monica hooked a Snickers bar, I got a plastic dinosaur, and Regis got a card with a hair bow on it. He kept staring at Monica's Snickers bar until she finally traded with him.

You entered the House of Horrors through a refrigerator carton with a hole cut in the front. It was painted up to look like a cave.

"I'll go in first," I said. "Since I'm the oldest."

"Me next," Monica said. "It's mor'n likely all fake."

"I don't want to be last," Regis said. "Put me in the middle."

"Oh, all right," I said. "Hold onto the back of my coat."

A voice that sounded like Junior Varsity Coach Bryant trying to sound spooky said, "Only the strong at heart may enter here. The last kid that came through had a heart attack and had to be rushed to the hospital."

We found ourselves in a narrow tunnel with black curtains on both sides. The only light was a flashlight that Coach Bryant was holding under his chin. He had on a ghoul's mask and big plastic horror hands. Even in that light, I could see that he was wearing his letter jacket from East Texas State. With his free hand, he was holding a bowl.

"Put your hand in here, if you dare," he said. "This bowl contains human eyeballs taken from criminals executed at the state prison in Huntsville."

I stuck my hand in the bowl, then jerked it out again. Regis stuck his hands behind his back and wouldn't try. When Monica put her hand in, she said, "Oh, foot! This ain't nothin' but a bunch of peeled grapes."

"Follow me to even more horrible horrors," Coach Bryant said. "Observe what I have in my hand now." He was holding a square basin out of the chemistry lab. "It is the blood of hospital patients who died of the gallopin' consumption, which is very contagious."

I stuck the end of my finger in and immediately wiped it off on Grandpa Weatherford's old coat. It sure felt like blood ought to feel. I couldn't be sure on account of I'd never felt any.

Regis looked sick and grabbed onto me even tighter than before.

Monica stuck two fingers into the basin, then smelled them. "Strawberry Jell-O," she said.

"The spirits of the dead don't like smart-alecky little girls," Coach Bryant said in his own regular voice. Then I guess he remembered where he was and went back to his fake spooky voice. He reached behind him and came up with a wooden fruit bowl. For just an instant, he shined his light on it. "And last, but not least," he said, "we have the guts of Vance Dalrymple, the notorious serial killer from Corpus Christi."

Me and Regis passed on that one. Monica walked up, stuck her hand in the bowl, and pulled something out, something long and limp. I like to of died when I saw what she did next. She popped it into her mouth.

"Umm, gummy worms," she said, "my favorite."

I'm sure glad I'm too young to be on junior varsity. I'd sure hate to meet Coach Bryant on the practice field on Monday. His spooky voice sounded like he was dressing down the players in the locker room after they'd just lost the most important game of the year.

"That ends the House of Horrors," he said, opening the flap at the back of the booth. "Pleasant dreams, children. Heh . . . heh . . . heh. Come on, move it! We ain't got all night."

When we came around to the front of the booth, I heard someone banging on the piano, telling me that the cake walk was about to begin. Folks were already lining up for tickets, and I could see Mr. Thripp holding up Willie Mae's cake for everyone to see.

"I gotta go do the cake walk," I said.

"Uh-uh," Regis said, "bobbin' for apples is next. We're working our way all around. Remember?"

"I'm doin' the cake walk. Y'all can do what you want to," I said.

"Come on, baby. I'll bob with you," Monica said. "Git on over there, J.R. If you win that cake, we can take it camping with us."

I was the last one to pay my dollar and get in line. The piano was playing "I'm an Old Cowhand from the Rio Grande." When the music stopped, Butch was the one left without a chair, so he had to leave. He grinned and waved at the rest of us. The next one to leave was Mr. Popolus from the Owl Cafe, then Mrs. Muckleroy's husband, Curtis. Finally, no one was left but me and Reverend Poteet. He patted me on the head.

"I sure could use that cake, J.R.," he said. "You get to eat Willie Mae's cooking all the time."

"The best man wins," I said.

When the piano started playing again, it played "Dixie," which is a pretty fast tune. Me and the reverend were almost running around the one chair that was left in the middle of the space. The music stopped, and just as Reverend Poteet was about to beat me to the chair, he slipped on a nacho someone had dropped and fell to the floor. While he sat there rubbing his behind, I slipped into the chair. He stood up and stuck his hand out for me to shake.

"I reckon the Good Lord meant for you to win," he said, "but you owe me one, J.R. You have to invite me to your house to share in your booty."

I just grinned and didn't tell him that this cake was headed for a camping trip. I took the cake from Mr. Thripp and carried it to the bingo table, where Biggie was sitting with Miss Lonie and some of the Daughters. The reverend followed and dropped into a chair next to Biggie. I found a folding chair and pulled it up between them. Me and the Reverend Poteet were both breathing hard from the cake walk. Biggie pushed her four bingo cards aside and turned to talk to the reverend.

"Reverend," she said with a big grin, "something just this very minute popped into my mind. I wonder if you'd be offended if I asked you a question."

"Of course not, Miss Biggie," the reverend said, giving her his full attention. "Ask away."

"It's just my curiosity," she said, "but where did you go to seminary?"

"The Episcopal Theological Seminary at Austin," he said, looking sort of puzzled. "Why do you ask?"

"Oh, nothing," Biggie said, "it's just that I can't help being curious about people."

"Well, nice losing to you, J.R.," the reverend said. "I think I'll wander over and have me one of those candy apples at the lovely Daughters' booth. Good night, Miss Biggie."

I watched as he walked toward Meredith Michelle's booth real slow, stopping to examine something at the other booths every now and then as if he might just change his mind. Meredith Michelle was watching, too. Her face lit up like a street lamp when he finally made it to her booth and leaned across the counter to whisper something in her ear.

I was getting ready to go and find Monica and Regis when someone dressed as Glenda, the Good Witch of the East, came and took a chair right next to Biggie.

"Gimme five cards," the witch said to Mr. Plumley, who was working the bingo booth for the Lions Club. "I feel lucky tonight."

" 'Evening, Butch," Biggie said. "You look downright lovely."

Butch smoothed his pink net skirt. "I know," he said. "Have you found out anything about Monk's murder? Everybody in town's talking about it."

"Yeth," Miss Lonie said, "I heard he was thmuggling

drugth and some gangsters from Tyler came down and thmoked him."

"Smoked him?" Biggie asked.

"That wasn't what they did," Butch said. "What they did was, they took him out to the equipment yard and ran him over with a bulldozer, then left his body back at the funeral home."

"Butch," Biggie said, "will you please be quiet? I just missed that last call. Was it I-Nineteen?"

I nodded.

"Bingo!" Biggie yelled, like Monk's murder was the last thing on her mind.

"Rosebud's at the door," Monica said, coming up behind me. "He says we got to get on back if we're figuring on going camping with him."

"Where's Regis?" I asked.

"Right over there sitting with his mama," she said. "He has to watch her play bingo for the rest of the night because he spilled red punch all over his clown suit."

"Let's go," I said, giving Biggie a hug and grabbing my cake.

"Now, J.R.," Biggie said, "I want you to look out in the garage and get Great-Uncle Carbuncle Wooten's buffalo rug. It'll keep you nice and warm."

"That thing stinks, Biggie," I said, "and it's more'n likely got spiders in it."

"Well, shake it out real good then," she said. "And I don't want you kids to get out of Rosebud's sight. You hear?"

"Why, Biggie?" I asked. "We'll just be on Wooten Creek."

"I know," Biggie said, "but Rosebud's taking you to the far side of the creek."

"Yeah," Monica said. "My Uncle Walker saw a bear over there last year. He would of shot it, too, only his gun jammed."

"Well, I'm not sure about the bear," Biggie said, "but just don't stray far from Rosebud."

"What if I have to go to the bathroom?" Monica asked.

Biggie grinned and gave her a hug. "Well, just for that," she said, "but stay close by."

12

When we got outside, I didn't see Biggie's car anywhere. Rosebud led us to an old rattletrap truck that wasn't really a truck at all. It was a black '57 Caddy that had had the backseat cut out to make a truck bed. A homemade camper covered the bed. I saw a sign painted on the door of the truck. It said TYREE'S BAIT SHOP—LIVE WORMS AND MINNOWS. Rosebud answered my question before I had time to ask. "We're taking Tyree's truck on account of we're going 'way down to the creek bottom, and I sure don't want to get Miss Biggie's car stuck in the mud."

When she sat down on the old quilt that covered the seat, Monica held her nose. "Oowee," she said.

"Never mind, youngun," Rosebud said. "We'll just roll down the windows and air this here vehicle out."

Willie Mae was bustling around the kitchen getting our food ready. " 'Bout time," she said as she packed a dozen apricot fried pies into a shoe box.

"Guess what, Willie Mae," I said.

"No need to guess," she said, not looking around. "You done cake-walked my chocolate cake right back home."

"Oh, I forgot," I said. "You know everything. How do you do that, Willie Mae?"

Willie Mae just looked at me and took a plate of fried chicken out of the fridge and set it beside the mountain of pimiento cheese sandwiches on the drain board.

"Woman, what you doin' with all that food?" Rosebud asked. "We aim to live off the land, catch fish, and shoot us a few squirrels, don'cha know."

"Uh-huh," Willie Mae said as she produced a dozen deviled eggs wrapped in plastic wrap. "Y'all better hightail it upstairs and get that makeup off of yourselves unless you plan to scare the daylights out of some rabbits and armadillos out there in them woods."

When we came back down dressed in long johns under our jeans and wool shirts, Willie Mae was packing the ice chest. "Y'all want Kool-Aid, or tea?" she asked.

Me and Monica said Kool-Aid and Rosebud said don't forget the coffee.

After we had all our gear and Willie Mae's food loaded into the back of the truck, I remembered something.

"I gotta get Uncle Carbuncle's buffalo rug out of the garage," I said. "Biggie says we might need it."

I looked where Biggie always kept it, hanging over the garage rafter and covered up with a tarp to protect it from spiders and dirt dobber nests. The tarp was right where it always was but the rug was gone, just vanished without a trace. I hated to tell Biggie. She sets quite a store on family heirlooms. I gotta admit, though, I was so excited about our camping trip that I forgot all about that buffalo rug until much later.

"Where we going, Rosebud?" I asked once we were rattling down the road in Tyree's old truck.

"Wellsir," he said. "First we're goin' past the family graveyard, then down past our fishin' spot, but we ain't stoppin' there. I happen to know of a low-water crossing further down the creek where we can ford across. We're settin' up camp on the other side of Wooten Creek."

"Hot dog!" I said. "Biggie never let me cross to the other side in my whole life. She says there's quicksand and wild hogs over there."

"Reckon she's right," Rosebud said, "that's why we're gonna have to be mighty careful."

"Haunts, too," Monica said. "I seen their lights in the woods once. Most likely, that's where the Wooten Creek monster has his den."

"I know a dandy camping spot," Rosebud said. "It's smack-dab in the middle of a clearing in the woods. Can't no Wooten Creek monster get us there lest we see him comin' first, and I got my shotgun loaded with monstershot." His shoulders shook, and I knew he was laughing that silent laugh of his. "Best part is, them trees are full of the fattest squirrels you ever laid a lip around."

After we drove past the Wooten family graveyard, Rosebud eased the old truck down the hill to the banks of Wooten's Creek then drove alongside the creek for about a mile before turning the truck right into the water.

"Whoa," Monica said. "What you tryin' to do? Drown us?"

Rosebud was holding tight to the wheel and staring straight ahead. "Don't get in a swivet," he said. "This here water's no deeper than your ankles."

When we finally drove out of the water, we found ourselves in a shallow draw just wide enough to let the truck through.

"What's this, Rosebud?" I asked. "It looks pretty near like a little bitty road."

"This here's the Trail of Tears," he said, pulling the truck into a wide clearing surrounded by tall pines. "Come over here and I'll show you something."

The moon was high overhead and real bright, a harvest moon. We followed Rosebud to the edge of the little draw and he pointed to a group of bushes about as tall as my shoulder.

"Shoot," Monica said. "Them ain't nothing but Cherokee roses. I see them growing all over these woods."

"The Indians planted them," Rosebud said, "back when the government drove them off their land. They planted them so the ones coming along behind would know the way. This here's the Cherokee Trace and it's tramped down like it is from all them Indian moccasins leaving the only home they ever knew. If you listen real careful, sometime, on a quiet night, you can hear their ghosts moaning and crying for their homeland."

We didn't say much as we pitched the tent and built a fire from some dried tree limbs we found in the edge of the woods. Finally, Monica said, "I know what we can do, let's sing songs around the campfire. I know all the verses to 'Polly-Wolly Doodle' and 'My Darling Clementine.' "

"Well, I'm not singing those old hokey songs," I said. "How about 'Ninety-nine Bottles of Beer on the Wall'?"

"How about we eat?" Rosebud suggested.

So we laid out the food and stuffed ourselves until we were too full to think about singing.

"I know what!" I said. "Rosebud can tell us a ghost story."

Rosebud scratched his head. "Lemme see," he said. "I could tell the one about the headless insurance man. He kept his head in his briefcase and, when he wanted to make a sale, he just set it on the table and his briefcase did the talking for him. He was right successful, don'cha see, because his prospects all wanted to get him outta their offices."

"Quit kidding," Monica said. "We want a real spooky story."

"Okay," Rosebud said. "See them tracks over there in that sand?"

"Sure," I said. "They're hog tracks. They're all over the place."

"That's right," Rosebud said, "and them is some fierce hogs, and don't you forget it. Now, I'm gonna tell you about the time the hogs ate old R. B. Debenport. See that stand of switch cane over there? Wellsir, that's exactly where it happened."

"Ooh," Monica said.

"Tell," I said.

"Well, it taken place along about 'thirty-two or thereabouts." Rosebud pulled out one of his smelly old cigars and lit it with a twig from the fire. "Back in them days, they still had stills around here where they made unlicensed whiskey. Seems like a well-known bootlegger had buried his whiskey money in a syrup can somewhere along this here creek bank and then went and got hisself kilt by a rival bootlegger. Hand me one of them deviled eggs, why don'cha?"

"I know," said Monica, "his ghost still roams the area."

"Might be," Rosebud said, "I ain't never heard nothing about it if he does."

"Then what's the story?"

"The story has to do with old Miz Finchner and her two redheaded boys, Ernest Ray and Delbert. See, them Finchner boys heard about that bootlegger's syrup bucket and thought they'd find it so they could take care of their mama, who made her living doing taxidermy work, which was hard on her on account of she was getting right old."

"Did they find it?" I asked.

"Well, no, on account of there was somebody else doing

some looking on their own. That somebody was R. B. Debenport, a sorry feller if there ever was one and two shades meaner than the devil hisself. Well, one night old R.B. found them Finchner boys diggin' around that sand bar where we crossed over the creek. He shot um both deader'n a six-card poker hand."

"What happened to him? Did they hang him?" Monica asked.

"Nope. Reckon he'd have preferred it if they had," Rosebud said. "Naw, old R.B. hightailed it out of town on account of he knew if the laws didn't get him, Mrs. Finchner would. He would have got away with it, too, if he hadn't been so greedy. That feller just couldn't stop thinking about that syrup bucket full of money still buried along Wooten Creek. A year later, he come slinkin' back into town. Taken hisself a room over at Miz Oterwald's boardinghouse. Started in sparkin' Lodema, the gal that did maid's work for Miz Oterwald."

"When's this story gonna get scary?" Monica asked. "I ain't got goose bump one on me."

Rosebud ignored that. "Well, first chance he gets, R.B.'s down at the creek with a shovel digging all over the place. Pretty soon, he's worked up a sweat and stops to get a drink of water. That's when he happens to glance over into the woods. What should he see, but two redheaded faces lookin' out at him, white as sheets and grinnin' to beat the band. Well, old R.B. don't do nothin' but hotfoot it back to town all ready to forget all about that syrup bucket. He wasn't too brave, don'cha know."

"I know, it was the ghosts of the Finchner boys," I said.

"Ain't you the smart one, though," Monica said.

"That ain't all the story," Rosebud said. "R.B. had done got right fond of Lodema, so he decided to stay on in Job's Crossing and maybe get married and settle down. Only

99

thing was, everywhere he'd go, he'd see them two white-faced redheads grinnin' at him. Finally, one fine day, him and Lodema decided to have a little picnic down here on the creek bank and, as you might have guessed, he strolled off to pick his little honey a bunch of bluebonnets when up pops them two faces again, leering at him from behind a sycamore tree. Well, if he'd been thinking rational, he wouldn't of done it, but old R.B. run fast as he could right smack into a stand of switch cane even through everybody knows that's the very favorite resting place for wild hogs in the heat of the day. Them hogs must of counted themselves awfully lucky to have their lunch delivered to them like that, because when they got through with R.B. there wasn't nothing left but his belt buckle and his pocket watch."

"So is this place haunted by the ghosts of both Finchner boys and R.B.?" Monica asked.

"Shoot no," Rosebud said. "Just R.B. What had happened was, old Miz Finchner had gone and taxidermied them boys' heads and mounted them on broomsticks. Then she just followed old R.B. around and made sure he'd see them heads ever'where he went."

"Boy, that was a smart old lady," Monica said. "What ever happened to her?"

"They tell she found that bootlegger's syrup bucket and moved over to Jefferson where her sister lived," Rosebud said. "Built her a nice little house and lived to be one hundred and six years old." He looked at his watch. "My, oh, me," he said, "we'd best be goin' to roost if we aim to be up in time for the fish to be having their breakfast."

"Rosebud," I said, "do you reckon those hogs might bother us?"

"Not unless you decide to go bargin' in on their afternoon nap," he said. "Mostly, they're scared of folks just like all wild critters are."

13

While we were dousing the fire and putting away the food, it occurred to me that this place wasn't a bit like the other side of the creek. For one thing, it was lowland and must of flooded quite a bit because a lot of the trees had died from root rot. Where the other side was soft and grassy, here the ground was bare and rocky and mushy in spots. Behind our campsite, the woods were dark as the inside of a cow. The wind had come up right smart. And cold? I felt goose bumps rise up in places I didn't know goose bumps could grow.

Rosebud put the ice chest in the back of the truck and pulled out a Coleman lantern. "You younguns grab your bedrolls and get in that tent," he said, " 'fore this here wind turns your innards into Popsicles."

Me and Rosebud hung a sheet down the middle of the tent so Monica could have her privacy. When we were all zipped into our sleeping bags, Rosebud turned out the lantern.

"I'm cold," Monica said.

"You'll get warm directly," Rosebud said. "Just lay real still."

"How 'bout another story," I said. "A funny one this time."

Rosebud yawned. "I'm plumb out of stories," he said, "and wore to a frazzle. Y'all just go on to sleep now. I'm done through messin' with you."

I'd never in my life seen Rosebud cross, so I figured I'd best shut my mouth and try to sleep. It wasn't easy, though, because the sound of the wind whistling through the trees made me think of those poor Indians moaning for their homeland.

Pretty soon, Rosebud started snoring like a freight train.

"Well, shoot a bug," Monica said. "Who could sleep with that goin' on. Heck, I already got a bad case of the big-eye from that dern story he told."

"Me too," I said, "but we got the biggest part of the night ahead of us. We'd best try to get some sleep."

I put my head under the covers to shut out the wind and curled up into a ball. Directly, I got warm, but just as I was about to doze off, I heard a voice from the other side of the sheet.

"I gotta go to the bathroom."

"Go," I said.

"By myself?"

"Of course, by yourself. I ain't goin' to no bathroom with a girl."

"Please, J.R.," she said. "You can stand in front of the tent, and I'll go around back. If you don't, I'm gonna stay right here and pee in my pants. I'll do it. You just watch and see."

"Okay," I said. "Come on, you little sissy-baby-can't-even-go-to-the-bathroom-alone."

"Call me anything you like," she said, "just come on!"

I stood in front of the tent, hopping up and down and slapping myself to keep warm for a plenty long time. "Ain't you through yet?" I called.

"J.R.," she called. Her voice sounded funny.

"You through?"

"J.R., come here. Hurry!"

I hurried to the back of the tent and found Monica looking off into the woods. "Look," she said. "Just keep looking."

I stared into the woods, but all I could see was blackness.

"Keep starin'," Monica said.

Then I thought I saw something, but wasn't sure. It was a stirring, like when you close your eyes for a long time until you start to see shapes moving behind your eyelids. I stared some more and it happened again.

"I think it's your eyes playing tricks," I said. "Come on back in. I'm cold."

"Wait," Monica said. "Keep starin'."

Suddenly I saw what she meant. A tiny pinpoint of light was bouncing like a rubber ball away back in the woods.

"Look! It's coming closer!" Monica whispered.

Sure enough, the light was getting brighter, then brighter. It was coming toward us.

"I'm calling Rosebud," I said.

Monica grabbed me by the arm. "No, we've got to stay here and watch."

As the thing came closer, I could see that it was moving fast and walking kind of stiff-legged. We could hear limbs snapping as it crashed through the underbrush.

"I see it," Monica yelled before I could clap my hand over her mouth.

"Be quiet," I hissed. "You want to get us killed?"

Then the thing cleared the woods, running along the edge of the clearing. It must of been nine feet tall and was all covered with fur. It carried a light in one hand.

"A bear!" I whispered. "Oh, my gosh. There's bears out here."

"Bear my hind foot," Monica said. "J.R., did you ever in your life see a bear walking on two legs and carrying a flashlight?"

"Well," I said, "grizzlies walk on their hind legs, but I can't say I've ever heard of one carrying a flashlight."

By now the creature had disappeared down the Cherokee Trace. I let out a sigh of relief. "It's gone," I said.

"J.R., you know very well what that was. That was the Wooten Creek monster," Monica said. "I ain't going to sleep one wink tonight."

She was wrong. That girl snores louder than Rosebud. Between the two of them, I like to never got to sleep.

When we woke the next morning, the sun was shining through the tent flap, and we could smell coffee brewing. Rosebud was sitting by the fire flipping pancakes.

"Some campers y'all are," he said. "Them fish prob'ly done had their breakfast and gone to take their naps."

While we ate our pancakes and bacon, we told Rosebud what we'd seen the night before.

"Most likely, there's tracks all over the place," Monica said. "Soon's I have one more of them pancakes, I'm goin' lookin' for them."

"Me, too," I said.

"Okeydokey," Rosebud said. "Reckon I'll just meet you two down by the creek bank, then. But first, head on over to that spring and draw up a bucket of water so we can wash up these dishes."

I picked up the bucket and we headed toward the spring. It was just a little shallow pool, no mor'n a hole in the ground with rocks all around it, but we could see clear water bubbling up out of the sand. After we'd filled the bucket, Monica pointed to the ground. "Look!" she said.

There in the soft ground next to the spring, I saw two giant footprints, exactly like the ones we'd seen at the graveyard.

"Jumping June bugs," I said. "Let's go get Rosebud."

Rosebud stood staring at the tracks for the longest time. Finally, he spoke. "Them sure ain't no pig tracks," he said. "Where else did you say you saw that thing?"

We all walked to the edge of the dark woods and, sure enough, more tracks made a beeline from the woods to the trace. And they must of been at least six feet apart.

When we got back to the camp, Rosebud sat down on a rock and poured himself a cup of coffee. "Way I see it," he said, "that there thing done come and left. Ain't a reason in the world why we can't get a little fishin' done, fry up our catch for lunch, then head on back to town. Whatchall say about that?"

The sun had come out and last night's wind had turned into a nice breeze. I had to admit, the place didn't look near so spooky in the daylight. Still, I noticed Rosebud hadn't said a word about going into those woods to shoot squirrels.

First, we set out a trotline across the deep end of the creek, then we line-fished the rest of the morning. I caught three perch, Monica caught a little bitty bass, which she threw back, and Rosebud caught two goggle-eye and a nice bass.

"See there," he said, "didn't I tell you them fish wouldn't be biting so late in the day?"

Still, there was plenty for our lunch. Rosebud rolled them in cracker crumbs and fried them over the fire. Then he made corn dodgers out of cornmeal and water and fried them in the fish grease. I expect Mrs. Muckleroy would have turned up her nose at it, but it tasted mighty good to us. Afterwards, we all lay down on the grass and had a nap. By the time we woke up, the sun was getting low in the sky, so Rosebud said we'd better check our trotline and break camp.

If you've never run a trotline, you don't know what you're missing. It's like opening your stocking on Christmas morning. You never know what you'll find. This time, we got a big snapping turtle, a water snake, which was scary looking but not poisonous, and one big old catfish. Rosebud said a snapping turtle makes mighty good eating, but he cut the line and let this one go on account of if one bites you, it don't let go until it thunders and, like Rosebud said, there wasn't a cloud in the sky. He let the snake go, too. But the catfish he cleaned and packed in ice for Willie Mae to cook.

I looked at that fish while he was flopping around on the bank waiting for Rosebud to fetch his knife out of the truck. It reminded me of the fish Biggie caught a while back and put in the toilet to keep while she went to her bridge game. We had a maid named Codella at the time. She went in to clean the bathroom and saw that fish in the toilet and somehow got the idea that she'd seen the devil himself. She ran out of our house squealing like a pig under a gate and never came back. They tell she never was right after that. To my way of thinking, she wasn't all that "right" before, but how do I know? I'm just a kid.

"Y'all might just as well drop me off at home on the way back to town," Monica said. "I believe I've had enough excitement to last until I'm at least thirty."

"Reckon so," Rosebud said. "You got plenty of tales to tell your mama and papa, don'cha, kid?"

I thought I had plenty to tell Biggie, too, but that was a big disappointment. All she said was, "J.R., there is no Wooten Creek monster. I don't know what you saw out there, but I expect it was your mind playing tricks on you."

I don't know what it would take to convince Biggie that I know what I saw.

After supper, I took my bath without being told to and put on my pajamas and robe. Then I curled up on the couch next to Biggie, who was watching *Murder, She Wrote*.

"I declare," she said, "that Jessica Fletcher is a smart woman. She's almost as good as me."

I didn't think so, but didn't say anything, just put my head on Biggie's lap and fell asleep. She woke me at ten and said, "Scoot on up to bed, J.R. We've got a big day ahead tomorrow. It's work day at the museum. The whole town's pitching in to get the old depot and the lot behind it cleaned."

I fell asleep between Willie Mae's clean sheets and dreamed we had the Wooten Creek monster stuffed and on display in our museum.

14

Well, it's about time," Mrs. Muckleroy said when me and Biggie and Rosebud arrived at the old depot the next day. "We've been cooling our heels here for a good ten minutes."

"Good," Biggie said. "I'm glad you got some rest, because before this day's over, you'll feel like you pumped a handcar across Texas. We've a heap of work to do. Did everybody bring brooms and mops and rags?"

"I did," Butch said from on top of a ladder. "I thought I'd just start right in dusting the ceiling before we start on the floor."

Miss Julia was over in a corner talking to Mr. and Mrs. Thripp while Miss Lonie and the Oterwalds were having cups of coffee from an urn Mr. Popolus from the café had brought over. Several of the men had already started to work on the lot out back where the model farm was going to be.

"Biggie," said Butch, "when we get the whole thing cleaned up, I think we should paint it light aqua with peach trim. Don't y'all think that would be a real attention grab-ber?"

"It's a depot, Butch," Mr. Oterwald said. "We're painting it chicken-shit yellow with brown trim. Oh . . . excuse me, ladies."

"Ooh," Butch said, "those colors just make me want to urp."

"Me, too," Miss Mattie said, "but I guess we should be authentic."

"I don't thee why," Miss Lonie said, "after all, it'th not a depot any longer. I favor red with white trim."

Mr. Plumley spoke up. "That's right. Copy my drugstore. Just because I've had the only red building in town for thirty-seven years, don't let that stop you—"

"Don't worry, Dedrick," Biggie said. "We're not painting it red. Now, let's get all this stuff moved out of here before we start to clean. Where the heck is Vida? We need some muscle here."

Mr. Thripp spoke up. "That's an insult, Miss Biggie. We men—"

Just then, Miss Vida walked in wearing too-tight jeans and a T-shirt with ELVIS LIVES printed on the front.

"Good," Biggie said, "now we can get started. Mattie, you and Julia and J.R. start taking those boxes out of the storeroom. Just set them on the platform until we can go through them. Rosebud, you and Vida take the telegraph machine. The rest of us can take the chairs and tables out."

"What should I do, Biggie?" Butch asked.

"Get a bucket and start in washing the windows outside," Biggie said.

Butch looked at his hands and started to say something.

"Never mind," Miss Vida said. "I brought some rubber gloves from the shop. Here, try these on."

Once everybody had pitched in and done their jobs, it was

noon, so we all gathered around a big table on the platform and opened our sack lunches.

"Butch," said Miss Julia, "what news do you have on the murder of Monk Carter?"

"Not much, Miss Julia," Butch said. "You take those state officers, they don't tell a person a blessed thing."

"That don't theem right," Miss Lonie said. "You're our acting police chief."

"Aw, that's okay," Butch said. "My gracious, ain't I busy enough with the costumes and sets for the operetta? Why, I'm spending the biggest part of my time down at the parish hall. Anybody want one of these cheese straws? I made um just this morning." He passed the plate to Miss Lonie. "Hand these around why don'cha? And that Reverend Poteet, lordy mercy, he has been just so sweet and helpful. What do I care about that old crime?"

"How about you, Biggie? You got a news item for me?" Miss Julia asked.

"Sure," Biggie said, "just write that the murderer will be apprehended soon, and that Biggie Weatherford knows exactly who it is. J.R., why don't you run over to the Wag 'n' Bag and get us all a cold drink."

Naturally, everybody wanted something different, so I tore a piece off my lunch sack and wrote down all the orders. I don't see why they couldn't just have a Big Red like I did. They're the best.

When I got back and opened my sack, I saw that Willie Mae had put in ham salad sandwiches on homemade bread, made with boiled eggs, chopped celery, green olives, and lots of mayonnaise, the way I like it, with bread-and-butter pickles on the side. I dug right in and wasn't paying much attention to what the grown-ups were saying until Mrs. Muckleroy got so loud I had to listen.

"Well, I don't like him even if he is a clergyman," she was saying.

"Ruby!" Miss Lonie said. "I think he's just as thweet as he can be."

"Why don't you like him?" Miss Julia asked.

"Because I think he's toying with my Meredith Michelle's affections. That's why!" Mrs. Muckleroy said. "And he ought not to do that."

"Looks to me like Miss Meredith Michelle's doing the chasing," Butch whispered in my ear.

"Well, I must admit, he seems to have only a nodding acquaintance with *The Book of Common Prayer*," Mr. Thripp said, "the way he fumbles around trying to find the lessons."

"You're on the vestry, Norman," Biggie said. "What do you know about him?"

"Only that he asked the bishop to send him here," Mr. Thripp said. "We were lucky, I guess. Not many young fellers would want be stuck in a hole-in-the-road like Job's Crossing."

Lucky for Mr. Thripp, he was eating his pie and didn't notice the look Biggie gave him.

Still, her voice was even as she asked him her next question. "But Norman," she said, "what did the bishop say about him? Where was his last parish?"

"Some little town up in Arkansas," Mr. Thripp said. "Waldron, I think he said."

"Why did he want to come here?" Miss Julia asked.

"The bishop didn't say," Mr. Thripp said. "Mattie, if you don't want that piece of pie, I'll take it off your hands."

"I declare, Norman, I don't see how you stay so skinny," Miss Mattie said, shoving her pie over to him.

"Biggie, can I go over and help the men clear the lot?" I asked.

"Good idea," Biggie said. "Rosebud, you might as well go, too. We women can take care of cleaning this place up."

"I'll go, too," Mr. Thripp said, shoving his last bite of pie in his mouth.

"Not on your life, Norman," Miss Mattie said. "We need you here to dust the high spots. Butch will be using the ladder for washing the windows."

The lot behind the depot is bordered by a chicken-wire fence that is falling down. Rosebud just pushed over a rotting post and we walked right through. As we stood on the edge of the lot deciding what to do first, I heard a voice shout, "Git outta the way, you sorry polecats!"

It was old Mr. Threadgill riding his souped-up lawn mower. He was waving his toy pistol at us. Since he was bearing down on us going a good ten miles per hour, we naturally jumped out of his way.

Mr. Threadgill uses his lawn mower for transportation and rides it all over town wearing a cowboy hat and holsters with cap guns in them. Because he is so onery, I try to stay out of his way whenever I can.

"That old man gonna git hisself kilt one of these days," Rosebud said.

"Biggie says he ain't right, and we should make allowances," I said.

"Stayin' outta his way is the only allowance I plan on makin'," Rosebud said.

While Rosebud went to help some men cut down a dead cedar tree, I walked around looking for stuff on the ground. You never know what you might find on an old vacant lot. As I came around the corner of the foundation of the old burnt-down house, I spotted a circle of bricks about six feet across. Thinking it was an old flower bed, I started past it, then I noticed it was a hole in the ground. And that hole was filled up with junk: old broken crockery, rocks, an old slop jar like Monica's mama keeps under her bed at night, and a bunch of bottles, mostly half-pint whiskey bottles. Since there might be some good stuff in there, I found an old slate shingle and started pushing things around to see what was underneath. Sure enough, I hadn't dug long before I found an old-timey wooden top, the kind you have to spin with a string. I laid that aside and dug some more. The next thing I found was a rock that looked like it might have veins of gold in it. Boy, I thought, I'm gonna get rich. There's valuable stuff in here. The next thing I found was an old lady's handbag made out of navy blue leather with the strap missing. I threw that aside and dug some more. Before I was through, I had a teapot with just a little crack in it, a blue granite saucepan that was only chipped around the edges, and a man's watch chain that might have been real gold.

I took everything and put it all in the car, even the lady's purse on account of I thought Biggie might want to have the strap fixed and carry it with her navy blue church dress.

When I got back, Rosebud was waiting for me by the hole.

"What do you know," he said, "a old cistern."

"What's that?" I asked. "A trash dump?"

"Naw, son," Rosebud said. "You take back in the olden days, folks used to dig a hole in the ground to catch rainwater. Them holes was called cisterns. Why, I recollect the time my daddy decided to dig a cistern on our place in Saint Martin's Parish. Hell, every time he'd dig down, he'd strike water. Finally, he give up. Cisterns ain't much use in south Louisiana."

"Rosebud," I said, "I'm gettin' downright tired of you always tellin' me those made-up stories. Now, why in heck would anybody want to collect rainwater?"

"To wash their clothes and hair with, Mr. Smarty. Back in

them days you couldn't just go in the kitchen and turn on the faucet anytime you needed water. You just listen to old Rosebud. You might learn something once in a while."

That night, after supper, I showed Biggie what I'd found.

"I thought you might like to have this handbag," I said. "It might even be an antique."

"Well, aren't you nice," Biggie said. "Just pass it on over here and let me take a look at it. No, first go get a rag so I can wipe it off a little."

When I came back with the rag, Biggie scrubbed some of the dirt off the bag, then held it up to the lamp. "Genuine leather," she said, "heavy, too. Let's see what's inside."

She tried to open it, but the clasp was bent.

"Go get me the pliers out of the toolbox," she said. "I'm curious as a kitten in a new room, now. This thing's got something in it."

Biggie had to break the clasp getting that bag open, then she pulled out a funny-looking flat tin can. "What do you know," she said, "an old Prince Albert tobacco can. I haven't seen one of those in I don't know when." She flipped open the lid and, when she looked inside, her eyes got big as Frisbees.

"Would you looky here," she said, digging into the can with her fingers. "Just looky here, J.R."

She pulled out a wad of money. She dug down some more and pulled out another chunk of money. She piled the money on the table beside her chair and commenced digging down in that old bag some more. It was another of those funny little cans, and it was full of money, too.

"Come on, Biggie," I said, "let's count it."

"Wait," she said. "There's something else. It's an old-timey card case. See? And there's cards in it. One's an identification card. The ink's faded so, I can hardly read it. Bring

114

your young eyes over here and see if you can make out the name."

I held the card up to the light.

"I see the town," I said, "it says Sherman, Texas. Three-oh-six Patterson Street, Sherman, Texas."

"The name, J.R. What's the name?"

"Well, Biggie, it's written in old-timey writing. I can't make it out too good, but I think the first letter is an *L*. Yeah, that's it. Lucille."

"The last name. Can you make that out?"

I peered at the card some more. "It looks like a *T*. Tarker? Is that a name, Biggie?"

"Let me see," Biggie said. "Could it be a *P*, do you think?"

"Parker? You mean like that Ma Parker y'all have been talking about?"

"Could be," Biggie said. "Tomorrow we'll get Julia to find out what her real name was. In the meantime, let's count this money."

We counted nineteen thousand dollars.

"Biggie," I said, "these bills look funny. You reckon they're counterfeit?"

"No, J.R. They're just old-timey bills—from, maybe, the thirties."

"Oh, boy," I said, "I'm going to buy me a motor scooter."

"Oh no you're not!"

Biggie seemed to think that, if we didn't find the real owners, the money belonged to the museum, just because it happened to be on museum property when I found it. She's taking it to that Texas Ranger tomorrow so he can investigate whether it was stolen from some old bank somewhere. She wouldn't even listen when I explained to her about finders-keepers.

"Not another word," she said. "Time for bed. Tomorrow's a school day."

"Just one question?" I asked.

"One."

"Biggie, you told all those folks today that you knew exactly who killed Monk. Was that the truth?"

"No, son, that wasn't exactly the gospel. It was what you might call strategy. It never hurts for folks to think you know more than you do. Now, up to bed and not a word about what I just told you."

15

The next day when I got home from school, I found Biggie and Willie Mae in Biggie's bedroom. They had taken every single thing out of Biggie's closet and piled it on the bed. It made a mountain of stuff. I didn't see how Biggie's little bitty closet had held it all.

"Biggie!" I said.

Willie Mae pulled a gray sweater out of the pile and held it up in front of her. "Miss Biggie, you're never gonna wear this again. Looky here, there's holes in the elbows and the pocket is tore half off."

"Let me see that," Biggie said. "I wore this to my first Daughters' convention in San Antonio in 'fifty-three." Biggie held the sweater out to her. "It's got sentimental value, Willie Mae. I just couldn't part with it."

"How 'bout these here slacks then?" Willie Mae said. "Looks to me like you lost right smart of weight since you last had these on."

"Oh, I was wearing those when I caught Old Bonehead,

the oldest and biggest catfish in Pine Lake back in 'sixty-one," Biggie said. "They're my lucky fishing pants, only I just can't wear them now." She held them up to her waist and I could see they'd wrap around her twice. "Who knows, I might gain a few pounds," she said and tossed them back into the pile on the bed.

"Biggie, I got—"

"Miss Biggie, you gotta get rid of some of this stuff," Willie Mae said. "Your closet looks like a rat's nest. Well, what about this then?" She was holding up a bright-colored skirt that was about the size of a dishrag.

"Oh, no," Biggie said. "That's my psychedelic miniskirt I bought in 'sixty-four. It's hardly ever been worn."

I heard Willie Mae say, "I'll bet!" under her breath.

"Biggie," I said, "I have to write a report about Arkansas for geography class, and I need you to help me. It's urgent!"

"We'll do it after supper," Biggie said. "That reminds me, I have to go down and talk to Rosebud."

I didn't know what my report had to do with Biggie talking to Rosebud, but I wanted to find out, so I followed Biggie out the door and down the hall.

Willie Mae stuck her head around the door and hollered, "Miss Biggie, you ain't goin' off leavin' this mess here!"

"You do it," Biggie said over her shoulder. "Pitch out what I don't need and keep what I do."

Willie Mae smiled, something you don't see very often. "Yes, ma'am!" she said.

I followed Biggie downstairs.

"Do you know where Rosebud is?" Biggie asked.

"Biggie, how would I know?" I said. "I just this very minute got home from school."

We found him in his little house having his afternoon nap. He near 'bout jumped a mile when Biggie pinched his toe.

"I didn't do it!" he yelled. "Oh, Miss Biggie, it's you." He sat up and rubbed his head. "I was havin' a dream. See, that there Wooten Creek monster was chasin' me. He'd got the idea I'd been messin' with his woman, y'understand, and he had it in his mind to get shed of me." He grinned. "Hotamighty! That female Wooten Creek monster was plumb eat up with the uglies."

"Rosebud," Biggie said, "remember when I sent you over to Shreveport to the Prudhomme Laboratory?"

" 'Course I do," Rosebud said, "I had to take that poor little dead dog with me."

"Well, I've got another traveling job for you. It's important."

"Where 'bouts you want me to go?" Rosebud asked. "Washington, D.C.? New York City?"

"Not quite," Biggie said. "Ever been to Arkansas?"

"Oh, yes'm," Rosebud said. "I once worked in one of them bathhouses over in Hot Springs, passin' out towels to them old wrinkled-up rich folks. I was just a boy at the time." He laughed and slapped his knees. "A young kid shouldn't have to see something like that. Scarred me for—"

"You'll need to pack a bag," Biggie said. "This trip may take a few days. You're going to Waldron, then clear up to Eureka Springs, then back to Little Rock to see the bishop."

"Reckon you want me to do a little detectin' on that reverend," Rosebud said.

"Put on your shoes and come to my house," Biggie said. "I'll make some coffee and we'll have a cup while I tell you my plan."

I sneaked some cheese out of the fridge while Biggie's back was turned and went over to Mrs. Moody's garage to feed my four baby rats. By now I had them eating out of my hands. Their mama had gone off somewhere . . . or most

119

likely, got eaten by Booger. While I was feeding them, I had an idea. I would get my old guinea-pig cage out of the attic and keep them in my room where they'd be safe. I knew now was a good time to do it on account of Mrs. Moody had gone to Wascom to visit her son who is a good husband and provider (he drives a bread truck) and her daughter-in-law who is lazy and watches TV and smokes cigarettes when she should be cleaning the house.

With her gone, I could slip the cage in through the garage door without getting caught. I'd wait until dark, then sneak my rats up the back stairs while Biggie and Willie Mae were watching *Wheel of Fortune*.

When I got back to the house, Rosebud was out at his house packing for his trip to Arkansas.

"I'm going down to talk to the ranger," Biggie said. "You can come along if you'll sit still and act right."

"What does act right mean, Biggie?" I asked.

"It means don't butt in when grown-ups are talking. Now, come on. We have to walk because Rosebud is taking the car to Arkansas."

I was pretty glad about that. It meant I didn't have to ride anywhere with Biggie driving for a few days.

"Get me that old purse full of money," Biggie said. "Put it in a paper sack for carrying."

"Yes'm. How come we're taking it with us?"

"Because it's not ours until the authorities try to find the rightful owners," she said, "but you can bet your last nickel I'll be watching to make sure no funny business goes on. We need that money for our museum."

I love to smell the courthouse. It smells like cigars and paper and glue and that disinfectant they use in the bathrooms. I don't know why; I just like that smell. Also, when you walk in the door, you feel a cool breeze since there's doors on all four sides, and they are kept open in good weather. We went downstairs to the basement and stopped at a door that had DEPARTMENT OF PUBLIC SAFETY painted on the frosted glass.

" 'Morning, gentlemen," Biggie said as she pushed open the door.

John Wayne Odle, the trooper, took his boots off the desk real quick and Ranger Upchurch stood up to shake Biggie's hand.

"Well, Miss Biggie," he said, "we were just wondering what went with you. I figured you'd be down here every day helping us with this murder investigation."

Biggie perched herself on the edge of a straight chair, her legs dangling two inches from the floor.

"Don't you worry about me," she said. "I haven't been idle. Did your people get any prints off that iron soldier we found?"

"Only Monk's," the ranger said. "We never thought it was the murder weapon anyway. Hell, there wasn't a scratch on the body. The man was mashed to death. The question is: How?"

"More important: Who?" Biggie said. "When we find that out, the *how* will take care of itself. J.R., give me that paper sack."

Biggie took the sack and dumped the two tobacco cans on the ranger's desk. "Look inside," she said.

"Well, I'll be hog-tied," the ranger said. "There must be upwards of ten thousand in here."

"Nineteen thousand," I said. "Me and Biggie counted it." Then I clapped my hand over my mouth on account of I remembered what Biggie'd said about acting up.

She didn't seem to notice, though. You never can tell about Biggie. Sometimes I'll be being dern near perfect and she'll jump on me like a bass on a minnow, and the next time I'll be bad enough to drive a preacher to cuss and she'll just

121

smile and pat me on the head. After a while, Biggie and the ranger got to talking about autopsies and stuff and I got bored, so I decided to go outside and wait.

I was sitting on a bench watching a squirrel bury a pecan when Cooter appeared from behind a tree and sat down beside me.

"Whatcha doin', J.R.?" he asked.

"Watching squirrels," I said, moving away from him to get away from the smell.

"Where's your grandma?"

"In the courthouse talking to the ranger. And she don't like people calling her grandma. Her name is Biggie."

"Well, I didn't know," Cooter said. "Do you reckon your gran—Biggie would pay for me a milk shake?"

"Don't know," I said.

"Would you ask her?"

"She's busy," I said, wishing Cooter would go away.

"Hey, J.R.," Cooter said, "you ever see the Wooten Creek monster?"

"Well . . ." I didn't really want to get into a conversation with Cooter, but that Wooten Creek monster sure had me interested. "I thought I saw him once. And I've seen his tracks."

Cooter grinned a big snaggle-tooth grin. "That there monster could eat a kid like you up in one bite and have your Biggie for dessert."

"How do you know so much?"

"I seen him. Shucks, I see him all the time. We're neighbors." He turned and faced me. "He don't like strangers campin' out on his side of the creek."

A chill went through me, and it wasn't just what Cooter said. When he turned to face me, I saw DeWayne's St. Christopher medal hanging around his neck.

I didn't say anything, just headed back inside the courthouse to wait for Biggie.

Willie Mae had made stew for supper and, since it was just the three of us, we ate on trays in front of the television. That's when I told Biggie about Cooter.

"Well, well," she said. "I'll have to give that some thought. As far as the monster is concerned, I have told you he doesn't exist. I want you to forget all about that. And as for DeWayne's medal, he could have dropped it somewhere and Cooter just picked it up."

"But Biggie, what about—"

"Be quiet, now. It's time for *Wheel of Fortune*," she said.

That reminded me of something. I started up the stairs.

"Ain't you gonna watch?" Willie Mae asked.

"Uh-uh. I think I'll play my video games," I said.

I hurried up to the attic and found my old guinea-pig cage. It was pretty rusty, and the door was sprung, but I could fix that. I even found the exercise wheel and water bottle. I took it to my room and lined the bottom with old *Weekly Reader*s. Then I dug into my closet until I found Booger's carrying case that we use when he has to go to the vet. I grabbed that and headed down the back stairs. After swiping some cheese from the refrigerator, I slipped out the back door.

Mrs. Moody hadn't locked her garage door, she never does, so I slipped in and whistled softly for my rats. They recognized my whistle. Pretty soon I saw four little noses twitching from underneath an old footlocker. They saw the cheese and came running toward me. I popped the cheese into the carrier and, when they were all in, slammed the door.

Pretty soon they got real upset and started running

around and jumping all over each other. I guess it was because the carrier must of smelled a good bit like Booger. I can't say I blame them on account of Booger's been trying to eat them ever since they were born.

I hurried back into the house and let them out in the cage where they ran around sniffing the bars and trying to figure out a way to escape. After I talked to them a while and gave them some more cheese, they settled down a little.

Biggie came in to tell me good night just as I was filling their water bottle. I must of jumped a mile and near 'bout fell out when she walked in and saw those rats. But there's one thing about Biggie. You don't ever know how she'll react to things.

"Well, I'll be a second cousin to a monkey," she said. "Cute little rats. You be careful, now. Don't let them get loose in the house or Booger will have himself a banquet."

I named them Flash, Slasher, Crusher, and Bruiser.

16

I want all the sailors onstage," the reverend said, "and Miss Biggie, you be waiting in the wings for your opening solo."

It was the first time we'd practiced the play since Monk got murdered, and you could tell everyone was jittery just thinking about that night.

I scrambled up on the stage in the parish hall and took my place in front of the group of other sailors. I glanced over in the wings and saw Biggie standing there with a plastic pail on her arm. I had to admit, I was a little worried about Biggie. She's awful good at a lot of things, but singing's not one of them. I knew because I'd heard her practicing in the bathroom when she thought nobody was around. After we sang our opening chorus, Biggie came onstage as Little Buttercup swinging her bucket, which, on opening night, would be a basket full of junk she would try to sell to the sailors. I wasted my time being worried. Nobody even noticed that she was off key most of the time on account of she put on a powerful show. She gestured and wiggled and made funny faces so much that the rest of the cast was on their feet clapping before she even got through with her song.

The rest of the rehearsal was a little stumble-footed, what with the sisters and cousins and aunts arguing about who was going to be in front and Meredith Michelle singing that dopey duet with the reverend. The best part was when Mr. Thripp was onstage. He was so mad about having to take the part of Dick Deadeye that he looked mean enough to bite the head off a cottonmouth and spit out the eyes. Since Rosebud had gone to Arkansas, Butch took his place as the captain.

After rehearsal was over, we all sat around the tables in the parish hall while the altar guild served punch and cookies.

The Reverend Poteet stood at the head of the table and said, "Ladies and gentlemen, I think we have a hit on our hands."

"Lord a mercy, reverend," Miss Julia said, "we looked like a bunch of spooked heifers up there. Didn't a soul know what to do."

"I agree," Mrs. Muckleroy said.

Mr. Oterwald said we'd have better luck putting toothpaste back in the tube than putting on a decent performance in two weeks, which is when the play is set to open.

"I was only trying to be upbeat," the reverend said. "I'll admit we've got a few rough spots to work through."

"Changing the subject . . ." Butch began.

"Why in hell do you want to do that?" Mr. Thripp asked. "What are we here for? To put on a play, that's what."

"Now, Norman, park your tongue," Miss Mattie said. "Let's hear what Butch has to say."

Butch put his foot up under him so he'd sit taller and said, "I solved a case today."

"You didn't!" Miss Lonie said. "Aren't you a thmart boy. Do tell!"

"Was it Monk's murder?" asked Mrs. Oterwald.

"No, honey. The state boys are working that one," Butch said, trying to sound tough, which is pretty difficult when you're wearing hot pink capri pants. "This was a local matter."

"Spit it out, Butch," Biggie said.

"Well," Butch leaned in toward the center of the table. "Ya'll know Cloyd and Dymple Whisanant that live over on Post Oak Street?"

"Is he about seventy years old and jack-legged from drinking bad whiskey?" asked Mr. Plummer.

"And does his wife work at the school cafeteria?" I asked. I'd seen a worker there wearing a name tag with DYMPLE printed on it.

"That's them," Butch said. "Well, I was sitting in my office this morning. I guess it was about ten, working on some paperwork, don'cha know. You simply have to keep on top of that paperwork or it will just drown you."

"Tell the story," Mrs. Muckleroy said. "It's getting late and Meredith Michelle's got to have her beauty sleep."

"Aw, Mama," Meredith Michelle said.

Butch tossed his head. "Well, I'm trying," he said. He wriggled in his seat like a happy puppy. "So, anyway, the phone rings. I answer and who do you think it was?"

"One of the Whisanants?" Biggie asked.

"Right," Butch said. "It was Cloyd. And guess what! He called to say there'd been a robbery at their house. Well, I just locked up the office and took myself right straight over to Seven-oh-three Post Oak Street. Poor old Cloyd was awfully upset. He was just gimping around all over the place, couldn't even sit down to give me a statement."

"Cloyd always was nervous—ever since he come back from the War," Mr. Plummer said. "Takes pills for it."

"Well, anyway, I finally got a statement from him," Butch said. "Seems as though someone had come right into his house, in broad daylight, while he was home, and stole three pairs of dress pants, one pair being his Sunday ones."

"I alwath thed crime would come to Job'th Crawthing thooner or later," Miss Lonie said.

"I think it's already here, Lonie," Biggie said. "Did you forget we've got an unsolved murder?"

"Oh, well, I wath talking about burglary and robbery—thtuff like that," Miss Lonie said.

"Oh," Biggie said. "Well, go on, Butch. What did you do?"

"Well, first I took his statement, like I said. Then I went around interviewing suspects. Mr. Cloyd said those pants were laying on the cedar chest that very morning before breakfast because he'd seen them there with his very eyes. So, naturally, I asked him who'd been to his house that morning. He thought a minute then, directly he said, 'I'm kindly thirsty. You want some coffee?' I said I'd take some. He went to get the coffee—had to make a fresh pot because the breakfast coffee'd gone all black and yucky."

Miss Julia had taken out a little pad and was writing the story down for the paper. "I declare, Butch, you are blathering like a blue jay. I can't write all this down."

"Who's asking you to?" Butch said, looking hurt. "I'm the one telling this story. So, anyway, Mr. Cloyd said the only soul that had been to the house were some Jehovah Witness people, a young man and his wife. He said he had nothing else to do so he invited them in and they talked about the Lord for forty-five minutes or so. Only, Cloyd said, they don't believe in calling Him the Lord on account of his name is Jehovah. Did y'all know that? I didn't. Miss Lonie, could I possibly have some more punch?"

While Miss Lonie poured, he continued. "Well, I got a description of them. The lady was wearing a sort of dark blue dress and *no makeup*! Can you imagine? And the man had on dark trousers and a white shirt." Butch took a swig of punch. "Well, I hate to suspect religious people, even if they do have some strange ideas. I mean, my real name is Billy, but I don't mind being called Butch. Why should the Lord mind having a nickname or two? But they looked like prime suspects until Mr. Cloyd told me something else."

"What?" I said.

Butch talked real slow so we'd know it was important. "He said he'd seen Cooter McNutt hanging around pretending to be raking leaves for the Williamsons across the street. Well, then I knew I had my culprit. I mean, that Cooter'll take anything that isn't nailed down."

"So did you arrest him?" Miss Mattie asked.

"Not right away, Miss Mattie," Butch said. "Proper procedures must be observed in police work. Everybody knows that."

I was hoping Butch wasn't getting too attached to that job, because it was a cinch he wasn't going to keep it once someone qualified showed up.

"What I did next," Butch said, "was to track down those Jehovah's Witnesses. They were just down the street at Seven-fourteen. I could tell pretty quick that they were innocent on account of they were on foot and you can't hide three pairs of men's pants on your person unless it shows. So I let them go and set out to look for Cooter."

"Where was he?" Mr. Oterwald asked.

"Actually, he was inside the Dumpster out back of your store," Butch said. "Old Cooter swore he didn't have nothing to do with it, but I locked him up, just in case, and went on down to the school to talk to Mrs. Whisanant. By the time I got there they were in the middle of serving lunch, so I sat and talked to Lance Jeffries, the music teacher, until she was done."

"Could she shed any light on the case?" Miss Julia asked.

"Matter of fact, yes," Butch said. "After careful interrogation, I was able to determine that Mrs. Whisanant had taken Mr. Cloyd's pants to be dry-cleaned on her way to work. Case closed."

Butch looked so proud of himself that even Mr. Thripp kept his mouth shut, and not a person laughed, although a few had to cover their mouths.

"Fine work, Butch," Biggie said. "Reverend, could I have a word with you?"

Reverend Poteet followed us out to our car so they could talk privately, but all Biggie wanted to do was invite him to lunch on Friday.

"I heard you were right let down over not winning Willie Mae's cake at the carnival, so I thought we'd just make it up to you. I'll have her make another just like it."

"Miss Biggie, you've made me a happy man. One's own cooking can become humdrum in a remarkably short time. A taste from Willie Mae's kitchen would be the Lord's blessing."

"I take it that means you'll come," Biggie said.

"With tinkling bells," the reverend said.

When we got home, I ran upstairs to check on my rats. They were pretty nervous on account of Booger was taking his nap on top of their cage. I fed them, then went back downstairs to the kitchen where Willie Mae was making hot chocolate. Biggie had taken her shoes off and was sitting at the table.

"Let's have stuffed peppers," Biggie was saying, "and some of those purple-hull peas Coye Sontag brought us."

"How about buttered new potatoes with parsley and sliced tomatoes and cucumbers?" Willie Mae said.

"Perfect," Biggie said, "and the cake, of course. Is the cocoa ready?"

Willie Mae sat our mugs in front of us, then poured a little in Booger's bowl and diluted it with milk. Booger had followed me downstairs because, I guess, he knew there'd be hot cocoa. That's one of Booger's favorite things, but he can't have too much because Dr. Furr, the vet, says it's not good for cats.

"Biggie, why are you having the reverend to lunch?" I asked. "I didn't think you liked him that much."

"I don't like him much at all," Biggie said. "That's why I'm giving him lunch. I want to quiz him about his past. There's just something about that young man—I can't exactly put my finger on it. But for the first time in, maybe, her life, Essie Muckleroy may be right about something."

"She doesn't like him because of Meredith Michelle," I said.

"I don't think that's it," Biggie said. "Essie'd be glad for Meredith Michelle to marry a priest—if he was on the up-and-up. I think Essie senses that there's something wrong with him. So do I. Did you feed those rats?"

"Yes'm."

"Then up to bed. School tomorrow."

17

Rosebud came home around four the next afternoon while I was sitting at the kitchen table having an after-school snack of cookies and milk and talking to Willie Mae.

"Oowee," he said, "I feel like I've been rode hard and put up wet." He flopped down on a chair in the kitchen. "Pour me some coffee, hon," he said to Willie Mae.

Willie Mae didn't say anything, just poured him a mug of hot coffee then put three chocolate chip cookies still warm from the oven on a saucer and set it in front of him.

Biggie'd been resting in her room, but when she heard Rosebud's voice, she came into the kitchen.

"Did you find out anything?" she asked, taking a mug down from the cabinet.

Rosebud held up his hand while he swallowed the cookie he'd stuffed into his mouth. Finally, he said, "Yes'm, you might say, in a manner of speaking, I found out a good bit."

"Well, what?" Biggie said.

Rosebud leaned his chair back against the wall so it balanced on its two back feet. He pulled a cigar out of his shirt pocket and lit it, blowing a smoke ring my way.

"This whole thing puts me in mind of the time I used to be a private investigator for the Seek'n'Spy Detective Agency in Tupelo, Mississippi." He turned to Willie Mae. "Pour me a little more coffee, hon."

Biggie put her chin in her hands and waited.

"What I done was, I single-handedly located the missing heiress to the Royal Wonder Greaseless Pomade Company fortune. I'm working the night shift down at the office when this gorgeous light-complected lady walks in—"

"Rosebud," Biggie said, "what did you learn in Waldron?"

"Umm," Rosebud said, "well, first I spoke to the newspaper editor up there. He just barely remembered the rev, don'cha know, but he sent me over to talk to the feller that runs the barbershop and also happens to be the head man on the vestry of that there church. Mr. Grundish, I believe his name was. He had one of them signs in his shop that said he had the right to refuse service to anyone, so naturally, I let him know from the git-go that I wasn't enterin' his shop with tonsorial expectations, that I only wanted a little information about a certain young shave-tail priest." Rosebud laughed, showing his gold teeth. "Wellsir, he was cuttin' a little kid's hair at the moment and had his hands pretty full seein' as how this kid was fightin' him and yellin' for his mama loud enough to wake up the dead."

"Rosebud," Biggie said, "if you don't get on with it, I'm going to snatch you baldheaded!"

"Yes'm. Well, first of all, I said to him, did he remember a Reverend Poteet. Naturally, he said he did. Well, then I asks the feller what do he think of the rev, and he 'lows as how he guessed he was a fair-to-middlin' priest seein' as how he wasn't hardly dry behind the ears yet."

Rosebud's eyes rolled toward the coffeepot and, without saying a word, Willie Mae poured more in his and Biggie's cups then refilled the almost-empty cookie plate.

"And . . ." Biggie said.

"Only thing was, this feller says they thought it was a little strange the way the reverend just suddenly up'd and left town without hardly saying good-bye or nothin'."

"That's odd," Biggie said.

"Yes'm, that's what I thought," Rosebud said. "The church folks heard later that the reverend had told the bishop he felt a call to go minister to the folks in Job's Crossing, Texas. Mr. Grundish said his parishioners was right upset because they felt that Arkansas sinners were just as much in need of salvation as any Texas sinners—and maybe a little more so."

"Anything else?" Biggie asked.

"Yes'm, right smart, but my pipes are gettin' dry. I reckon a little dab of Willie Mae's muscadine wine might oil um up some."

Biggie got up and took two little bitty glasses off the top shelf of the kitchen cabinet while Willie Mae got out the wine.

"I might just join you," Biggie said. She looked at Willie Mae, who shook her head. After the wine was served, Biggie said. "Can we continue?"

Rosebud smacked his lips. "Umm-umm, that's mighty fine," he said. "Well, let's see. Where was I. Oh, yeah, I'd just left the barbershop and was headin' back to the car, when I thought I'd just stop in the café and have me a cup of coffee. Naturally, I got to talking to some more fellers, just to be sociable, don'cha know. Well, God bless a billy goat if Monk Carter's name didn't come up."

"You mean you asked about him," Biggie said.

134

"No'm. Hadn't even thought about it. One of them fellers in the café said had the others heard that old Monk had got himself killed. Seems he was well known around there as being a gambler and a all-around scoundrel. Used to run a Saturday night poker game for one of them high rollers from over at Hot Springs."

"Did he run a funeral parlor?" Biggie asked.

"I asked um about that," Rosebud said. "They dern near laughed me out of the place. Said Monk wasn't a undertaker to their knowledge. They said he'd been raised around there and hadn't ever been much of nothin' but trouble with a capital T. But, here's the good part. Rumor had it around there that our very own Reverend Poteet was up to his ears in Monk's gamblin' operation. Even held games in the parish hall of the church once or twice—late at night when the good folks were asleep in bed."

"So," Biggie said, "the reverend hears a sudden calling to minister to the souls in Job's Crossing, and not long after, the man he gambled with, and quite possibly owed money to, buys Larry Jack's funeral home and fills it with expensive antiques."

"And, Biggie," I said, "you remember when the reverend first brought Monk to your garden party? He seemed kind of nervous or—"

"You're right!" Biggie said.

"But, he couldn't have crushed Monk, Biggie. He ain't nothing but a little feller."

"Isn't," Biggie said. "And, you're right again. But sure as you're born, that preacher knows more than he's telling—and when he comes to lunch tomorrow, I intend to find out what it is."

"Get up out of that bed," Willie Mae said the next morning. "I got your breakfast ready, and here you ain't even up yet."

She glared at me. "Like I don't have enough to do gettin' ready for that reverend comin'."

"Ow! I got a sore throat," I said.

Willie Mae felt my forehead, then called Biggie into the room.

"He ain't got a speck of fever," she told Biggie. "He just don't want to go to school."

Willie Mae was right. I planned to stay right here to see what Reverend Poteet had to say for himself.

Biggie sat on the edge of my bed. "J.R., are you malingering?" she asked.

"Huh?"

"Are you just playing possum so you won't have to go to school?"

"No'm. I feel real bad. Honest."

"Have you got a test today?"

"No'm."

"Well, I haven't time to deal with you this morning," Biggie said. "Just stay up here in your room. I'll have Willie Mae bring you up some oatmeal for your breakfast."

I sat up in bed. "I believe I'll have pecan waffles," I said.

"Huh!" Willie Mae said as she went out the door. "Feller's got a sore throat, he don't need to be eatin' no pecan waffles. I'll bring you a poached egg."

I know when I'm beat. I read a library book while I waited for my poached egg.

When Willie Mae came back, she brought a poached egg on buttered toast with cream poured on top, fresh squeezed orange juice, and banana muffin. After I ate it all, I put the tray on the table, then sat on the floor and played video games. That got boring after a while, so I went to the top of the stairs and listened to what was going on below. I could hear Biggie and Willie Mae talking in the kitchen. I could smell Willie Mae's chocolate cake cooking.

"Biggie," I called. "Biggie, can I come downstairs?"

Biggie came to the foot of the stairs. "Not on your life," she said. "You want an aspirin?"

"No'm. I'm feeling lots better," I said.

Biggie's eyes narrowed. "Back to bed," she said.

I decided I might as well play with my rats. I opened the cage and pulled Slasher out. He's my favorite on account of he'll curl up around my neck and go to sleep. While Slasher was sleeping on my shoulder, I decided to let the others out to play. They climbed on my lap and ran around the room a lot. We were having a good time until Biggie came into the room. My rats all ran under the bed the minute they heard the door rattle. I hopped back into bed.

"Are you really feeling better?" Biggie asked.

"Oh, yes'm," I said. "I must of got well."

"Then get dressed and come downstairs," she said. "Put on some nice clothes. You can join us for lunch. I need your eyes and ears while I question the reverend."

By the time I got dressed, Biggie was letting Father Poteet in the front door.

18

"Come on in the house, Father," Biggie said. "Pull your coat off and give it to J.R., and we'll go straight in to lunch."

The reverend stuck his nose in the air like a cow dog sniffing a stray. "Gladly," he said, wriggling out of his coat.

We ate in the dining room. Biggie had spread the table with her mama's damask cloth that we only use for Thanksgiving and Christmas. The napkins are as big as dish towels. When Willie Mae brought in a big platter of orange peppers stuffed with ground veal and rice seasoned with lots of garlic and black pepper, the reverend reached out and started to pull the platter toward him.

"Reverend Poteet!" Biggie said in a loud voice.

The reverend looked at Biggie, still holding on to the platter.

Biggie bowed her head. "Would you please return thanks?" she said.

"Oh, my. Well, certainly. For what we are about to receive, make us, er—how does it go?"

"—truly thankful," Biggie said. "Let's eat."

I ate three stuffed peppers. One little poached egg for breakfast don't stay with you too long. The reverend ate four peppers plus three helpings of potatoes and six of Willie Mae's icebox rolls with butter. I wondered where he put it all, seeing as how he can't weigh much more than a hundred and thirty pounds.

After he sopped up the last of his tomato gravy with the last roll on the plate, Biggie pushed her chair back and stood up. She led the way into the parlor.

"I thought we'd just have coffee and dessert in here," she said, "but perhaps you'd rather wait a while?"

"Not me," the reverend said.

Biggie offered the reverend the wing chair and sat herself down in her favorite Boston rocker. She hadn't asked a single question during lunch, so I figured she'd go to work on him now. I was right. After Willie Mae had served the coffee and cake, she turned to face him.

"Reverend," she said, "the town's just buzzing about you."

The reverend smiled. "Why, Miss Biggie, I'm just a poor clergyman. What could they possibly have to say about me?"

"It's about Meredith Michelle Muckleroy. Will we be hearing wedding bells soon?"

The reverend blushed. "Oh, well, I don't—I mean, Meredith Michelle is certainly a fine-looking girl. But I . . ."

"The town's hoping you'll marry a local girl and decide to stay with us forever. We seem to have a hard time keeping clergy in Job's Crossing. They all want to go off and better themselves in bigger towns, don't you know."

The reverend relaxed. "Oh, no. I'm not like that. I want to serve the Church wherever I'm called."

"I believe I heard that your last parish was in Waldron,

Arkansas. Is that correct, Father?" she asked like she was making polite conversation.

"That's right."

"And how long did you stay there?"

"Only two years," he said. "It was a sad little place, I'm afraid. Quite poverty-stricken. They simply couldn't afford a rector. Now they share a priest with the congregation in Del Valle, Arkansas." He licked his fork and looked at Biggie with wide-open eyes. I could see he was trying to look like he was ready to tell Biggie anything she wanted to know. I've done that trick a dozen times when I wanted a grown-up to think I was telling the whole truth.

"More cake?" Biggie asked. Without waiting for an answer, she shoved another big slice onto his plate. "And why did you ask to be sent to Job's Crossing?"

For the first time, the reverend's eyes took on a little squint. "No, well, I'd never even heard of—why would I do that?" He looked down into his empty coffee cup then held it out to Biggie. "Could I, er . . ."

"J.R.," Biggie said, "take the coffeepot into the kitchen and ask Willie Mae to refill it."

As I was leaving the room, I heard Reverend Poteet say, "Mighty good coffee, Miss Biggie. These are awfully pretty cups, by the way. Is this your family crest?"

Normally, Biggie would be real glad to talk about her family crest, but not when she's sniffing out a mystery. "Yep," she said. "So you say you'd never heard of Job's Crossing?"

When I came back with the coffee, the reverend was saying, "Miss Biggie, did I happen to tell you what a smash you were at rehearsal? You are a natural actress."

Biggie couldn't keep a little smile from shoving up the corners of her mouth, but she didn't take the bait. "Waldron," she said in her best tea-party voice. "Seems to me we passed through there in 'eighty-seven when the Daughters had their retreat in Eureka Springs. I believe you said once that Eureka Springs was your hometown?"

Reverend Poteet relaxed a little. "Born and raised," he said. "In fact, it was through a summer job with the *Anglican Digest* up there that I was called to the priesthood."

Biggie smiled her sweetest smile and went in for the kill. "I'll bet your mama was proud," she said, reaching over and patting him on the knee. "Now, honey, I hope you'll forgive an old woman's curiosity, but in our investigation of Monk's murder, we found the oddest coincidence. We found that Monk Carter was actually living in Waldron, Arkansas, before he moved to Job's Crossing. Isn't that just the strangest thing? And to think you'd never met him."

The reverend sat up straight in his chair. "Miss Biggie, I don't know what you're implying . . ."

"Nothing. Nothing at all, honey. More cake?"

"Biggie," I said, "can I go to my room now?"

"Of course," she said. "Nobody's keeping you here."

I picked up Booger, who was napping on the back of the couch, and took him with me. That was a big mistake on account of when I opened the door to my room Flash, Slasher, Crusher, and Bruiser took one look at Booger and skedaddled out the door and down the stairs. Me and Booger followed as fast as we could, but can't nobody outrun a rat. Naturally, they headed straight for the parlor. Flash, Crusher, and Bruiser ran under Biggie's armoire and crouched there, twitching their whiskers. But Slasher ran up the reverend's leg and curled around his neck.

The reverend screamed and spilled his coffee all over Biggie's hooked rug that her mama had made. That must have scared Slasher, because he took a big bite out of the reverend's cheek. The reverend jumped up in his chair, and that's when he surprised me quite a bit. He let out a batch of cuss words like I'd never heard before. What he thought of my pet rats was sure enough X-rated. I stood there with my mouth open, not knowing what to do as he ran out the front door, forgetting to take his coat. I looked at Biggie. She had a strange little smile on her face.

"J.R.," she said, "you'd better catch those sweet little things and put them back in their cage. Then go out into the kitchen and see if Willie Mae has any of that good Swiss cheese left. I think they deserve a nice treat."

There's no figuring Biggie. I thought I'd be in big trouble, and there she was, smiling and rocking like she'd just had the time of her life.

"J.R.," Biggie said later, "I want you to ride your bike down to the Piggly Wiggly and get a can of red salmon. I feel like salmon croquettes for supper."

"You best get some saltine crackers and a dozen eggs," Willie Mae said.

I jumped on my bike and headed for the store. If there's one thing I like better than fried catfish, it's Willie Mae's salmon croquettes with plenty of catsup on them.

Just as I was rounding the produce aisle and heading for the eggs, I saw my teacher, Miss Fleming, pinching tomatoes. I ducked my head and started back the other way, but not soon enough.

"J.R. Weatherford!"

"Yes'm."

"Would you mind telling me why you weren't in school today, and now I find you sashaying around the grocery store?"

It took a while before I could convince her I was really sick this morning. She finally let me go but said she was calling Biggie tonight to see if I was playing hooky.

I finished my shopping and hung the sack over my handlebars. A Texas blue norther had blown in while I was in the store. I was pretty near blue myself by the time I got home.

Willie Mae was waiting at the kitchen door for me. "Get in here," she said. "Look at you, runnin' around in this cold without nothin' on but a T-shirt. You'll sure 'nough be sick tomorrow."

"But it wasn't—"

"Set down here. I made you some hot spiced tea," she said, wrapping a blanket around me.

"Ow! This tea's too hot," I said. "Where's Biggie and Rosebud?"

"Blow on it, and it'll cool down," she said. "They be havin' a private discussion, and it ain't none of you."

"Yes'm," I said. Willie Mae can be stubborner than Biggie when she wants to.

Just as I was finishing my tea and sweating like a plow mule, Biggie and Rosebud came into the room.

"You did a good job, Rosebud," Biggie was saying. "I just wish I knew why he wanted to be sent here."

"Yes'm," Rosebud said.

Biggie walked to the window and looked out. "Good Lord," she said, "we've had a norther blow in."

"It's cold," I said. "I'd probably have pneumonia right this very minute if Willie Mae hadn't wrapped me up real fast."

"Miss Biggie," Willie Mae said, "you got any way to heat that depot?"

"Lord, no," Biggie said. "It's been so hot this fall I guess nobody's thought of it. What should we do? It's a cinch we can't afford central heat—and space heaters are too dangerous."

"You could just open up when it's warm," I said.

Biggie ignored me. "Any ideas, Rosebud?" she asked.

143

"You bet," Rosebud said. "Over at Mr. Ike's House of Feed, they got these big old heaters hung up in the rafters with fans in them that blow the heat all over the place. I been in there in twenty-degree cold and it's warm as this here kitchen."

"How do they light them?" Biggie asked.

"Same as your furnace," Rosebud said. "They got thermostats on them."

Biggie stood up. "I'm calling Ike right this minute," she said. "I'll tell him to get his heater man down to the depot first thing in the morning."

Later, when I went to tell Biggie good night, I remembered something.

"Biggie," I said, "I ran into Miss Fleming in the store, and she said she was calling you tonight on account of she don't believe I was really sick."

"Doesn't," Biggie said.

"Huh?"

"She doesn't believe you were sick."

"Yes'm. Well, what are you gonna tell her?"

"That you were sick as a poisoned pup, and I might have to keep you home again tomorrow," she said.

"Really? You might?"

"Of course not, J.R. There's not a thing wrong with you." She grinned. "But you and your rats sure made that reverend show his true colors."

You bet," Rosebud said. "Over at Ma Ike's House of ---ed, they got these big old heaters hung up in the rafters ---fans in them that blew the heat all over the place. I been

19

Saturday morning, I'd planned to sleep late, but Biggie had other ideas. She sent Rosebud up to wake me.

"Rattle your hocks," he said. "Your Biggie's got things to do."

"I think I have a sore throat," I said.

"It's Saturday," Rosebud said, showing his gold teeth.

"Oh yeah. What's for breakfast?"

"Pancakes with apples and pecans with plenty of melted butter—and powdered sugar to sprinkle on top."

I had three pancakes with some little link sausages on the side.

"What we gonna do, Biggie?" I asked, scraping butter and powdered sugar off my plate with my knife.

Biggie was changing the stuff out of her big white summer purse to her big black winter purse. She had a pile about the size of Willie Mae's stew pot dumped out on the table. "We're going to the depot to see how that heat works," she said. "The workmen finished the job yesterday." She pulled something black out of the purse and looked at it like she'd never seen it in her life. "What do you suppose this is?" she asked. "Oh, well." She threw it back into the old purse.

"Lemme see that," Rosebud said. He held it up to the light. "It's either a wienie or a banana. I can't tell which." He tossed it in the trash.

Biggie shoved the last of the pile into her black purse and started for her room. "Get your coat on, J.R.," she said over her shoulder. "That wind will cut through you like a hot knife through butter."

"Biggie," I said when we were in the car, "can we go ask if Monica can spend the night? She ain't seen my rats or my new Nintendo."

"Hasn't," Biggie said.

"Oh yeah. Well, can we?"

"Sure," Biggie said, "but the two of you have to go with me to meet the Daughters for lunch."

"Not the tearoom!"

"Nope. We're going to the Owl today. You can have a piece of Popolus's good pie."

Monica was so excited at going to town she couldn't stop talking. As we crossed the railroad track, she said, "Them old trains are louder'n a windmill that ain't been oiled in a while."

"Hasn't," I said.

"Huh?" Monica said. "Miss Biggie, can't you do something about it? The dern Cotton Belt woke me up this morning."

"I've got no influence with the railroads, Monica," Biggie said. "Anyway, they only come through twice a day."

"Yes'm, I know, but they come at seven in the morning and eleven at night. I'm sleepin' then."

Biggie stopped the car. "So they do," she said.

She turned the car around and headed back toward the crossing. "We'll just take the tracks back to town. It'll get us there a good ten minutes sooner."

"Biggie, I don't know," I said, but it was too late. We were already bouncing along those railroad ties with Monica laughing her head off. Biggie was right, of course. We got to town faster than a bass can gobble a minnow.

It was good and warm in the depot. I looked up and saw two big gray heaters hung from the ceiling. They were blowing warm air right down on top of us. Mr. Oterwald was busy cleaning out some old boxes of depot papers while Mr. Peoples, who runs the Eazee Freeze, stood on a ladder slapping white paint on the walls in the telegraph room.

"I see Bertram's man did a good job," Biggie said to Mr. Oterwald.

"Too good," said Mr. Peoples from the ladder. "I'm hotter'n a two-dollar pistol on Saturday night. Any way to turn that thing down?"

"No, they ain't, Roy Lee," Mr. Oterwald said. "Them men set the dang thing to kick in when it gets to be sixty-five degrees in here, only the dern fools didn't stop to think that heat rises—and they got the gol-derned thermostats down there on the baseboard. Every time it gets sixty-five on the floor, them things kick off again."

"We'll get it fixed," Biggie said. "Meantime, Roy Lee, maybe you ought to paint down low for a while. And it might be a good idea for you to wear some other shoes. You're liable to fall off that ladder wearing cowboy boots."

Mr. Peoples came down off the ladder. "Reckon I'll just have to take my chances," he said. "A man ain't a man without his boots. Hey! I brought my guitar along. How 'bout a tune while I take a break?"

Biggie moved toward the door. "Sorry, honey," she said, "we've got a luncheon date."

As we got into the car, I could hear Mr. Peoples singing "Mule Train" real loud. I wondered how poor Mr. Oterwald could stand it.

When we got to the café, the ladies were all sitting around the big round table where Mayor Gribbons fell over dead in his cake last year. Even though I was there and saw the whole thing, it doesn't keep me from liking the Owl. It's a kind of dark and cozy place. The tables are covered in red-and-white-checkered plastic that Mr. Popolus just wipes up with a sponge if you spill anything. He don't even give you a dirty look like Mr. Thripp does. Hanging over the bar is a ferocious-looking old boar's hear that Mr. Popolus brought over from Greece when he was only eleven years old.

"Biggie," Mrs. Muckleroy shouted, "when do you suppose Itha Rae's getting back?"

"How should I know?" Biggie said. "I don't even know for sure whether she's ever coming back."

"Well, something's got to happen soon," Mrs. Muckleroy said. "Would you just look at Lonie's hair?"

Miss Lonie's hair was bright yellow—not blue like it usually is, and curled up so tight it looked like she had a soccer ball perched on the top of her head.

"Ye gods," Monica whispered to me, "she looks like she stuck her finger in a light socket."

"Vida did thith to me," Miss Lonie said. "I can't even get my Thunday hat on."

Monica like to turned blue trying to keep from laughing.

"I reckon it'll grow out," Miss Julia said. "But what about the rest of us? My hair's just sticking flat down to my head because I'm afraid to turn Vida Mae loose on it."

Biggie had been studying the menu like she wasn't listening. "I believe I'll have the plate lunch," she said. "Popolus has pork chops with candied sweet potatoes and green

148

beans today." For the first time, she glanced at Miss Lonie. "Lord a mercy, Lonie," she said, "let me get my glasses on. My stars, your hair's just plopped up on top of your head like a turd on a melon stalk."

Mrs. Muckleroy held her water glass up to the light to make sure it was clean, then wiped the rim with her napkin. "No need to be crude," she said. "But I have to admit, there's just no other way to describe Lonie's hairdo."

Mr. Popolus had been standing by our table waiting to take orders. Monica spoke up first. "I'll have the fried chicken basket with gravy instead of catsup. And a Big Red to drink."

"Me, too," I said.

That got the Daughters thinking about food, and pretty soon Mr. Popolus had started back to the kitchen with everybody's orders.

"By the way, Ruby," Biggie said, "how come you're hiding your hair under that scarf?"

"Because I'm ashamed to let anybody see it, if you must know," Mrs. Muckleroy said. "I was fool enough to let her give me a trim—a trim, mind you, not even a full cut."

"Let's see," Biggie said.

"Yeah," Monica said. "I'd sure like to see."

Mrs. Muckleroy glared at Monica. She don't believe in kids' rights. Looking like she'd just taken a bite out of a sour pickle, she slowly pulled the scarf off her head.

Everyone stared. Monica was the first to speak.

"Gol-ly," she said. "It looks just like a doll I once had. I left it outside for a whole winter. Buster thought it was his toy and chewed it up right smart. By the time I found it the next spring, its hair looked exactly like that."

"Well . . ." Biggie said. "I guess I could have a talk with Vida. Maybe she can shed some light on when Itha'll be back."

149

"She's got to be back soon!" Mrs. Muckleroy wailed. "The pageant's in January. Who's going to fix Meredith Michelle's hair? Itha's been practicing this whole year to get it right."

After lunch Biggie said, "We might just as well stop by the shop on the way home and have a talk with Vida."

Miss Vida had Prissy Moody up on a table and was drying her with a blow dryer. She does dogs when she's not busy with people's hair. Prissy looked embarrassed when she saw me walk in, and I don't blame her. Her coat looked almost as bad as Miss Lonie and Mrs. Muckleroy's hair.

"Vida," Biggie said, "turn that thing off a minute. I need to talk to you."

Miss Vida turned the dryer off and turned to face Biggie. "I reckon I can guess what you're here for," she said. "I aim to finish cleaning out the storeroom at the depot soon's I can get the time. Prissy, quit that scratchin' me! I'll turn you loose directly. We're near 'bout finished." She picked up a towel and mopped her sweaty face. "With Itha gone, I'm busy as a one-legged man at a butt kickin'."

"When do you expect her back?" Biggie asked.

"Miss Biggie, how'm I supposed to know?" Vida said. "You know Itha. She does just exactly what she wants to, and it don't matter who she puts out." Miss Vida sighed. "Truth is I ain't all that busy. Business has fell off a good bit lately."

"Hmmm," Biggie said. "You suppose you ought to get Davalene Marsh to come in and help out while she's gone?"

"Miss Davalene's too old, Miss Biggie," Vida said. "Only reason she retired in the first place was because of her corns. She just can't stand on her feet no more."

"Okay," Biggie said. "Well, you take care, Vida."

"You gonna be in for your standing appointment tomorrow?" Miss Vida asked.

"Nope," Biggie said. "You can scratch me off the appointment book indefinitely. I'm too busy with the depot to take time out for hair." She stood up. "Come on, kids, I feel a nap coming on."

As we went out the door, Biggie turned back to Miss Vida. "By the way," she said, "when you do get back to the depot, you'll be pleased to know we now have heat in there."

I don't think Miss Vida heard her. She'd already turned the hair dryer back on poor old Prissy.

Me and Monica played video games for a while. Monica wasn't too interested in my rats on account of she had a whole barnful at home, so we rode bikes for the rest of the day.

Willie Mae made Monica's favorite meal for supper: wienies and sauerkraut with french fries. After supper, me and Monica watched a space movie on TV then turned in early on account of we were worn out from bike riding. Willie Mae made Monica sleep in the guest room on account of it ain't fittin' for a big old half-grown girl to sleep in a boy's room.

Something woke me up around eleven. I laid real still and listened. It was a sound far off. I couldn't quite make out what it was. I went to my window, opened it, and stuck my head out. Then the sound came clear. It was the fire alarm. I leaned 'way out the window so I could see better. What I saw made me run to Biggie's room.

I shook her. "Biggie," I hollered. "Biggie, wake up!"

Biggie don't like being waked up. "This better be good, J.R.," she mumbled.

"Biggie, get up!" I said, grabbing her hand. "The depot's on fire!"

20

After it was all over and the grown-ups had gone to bed, me and Monica sat up in my room most of the night talking about what had happened.

"Wow, you're lucky you live in town," Monica said. "Don't nothing like this ever happen in the country."

"Yeah," I said. "Did you see those flames, the way they shot up in the air? It's a good thing no airplanes was flying over. I bet they'd of caught on fire and fell right smack on top of us."

"Does everyone in town come to watch every time y'all have a fire?" Monica asked. "Shoot, it was kinda like a party out there."

"Mostly," I said. "You can hear the fire siren all over town. They got it mounted on top of the fire station to call in the volunteer firemen."

I remembered the scene when Rosebud had pulled Biggie's car into the parking lot. Cars and pickups were all over the place. Folks stood around in little groups talking to each

152

other and comparing this fire to the ones they'd seen in the past.

"Hell fire," Mr. Handy said, "this ain't nothin' next to when the old cotton barn burned. That thing was full as a tick on a dog's rear. Cotton bales, don'cha know. And, that blamed cotton smoked up the whole damn place. Why you couldn't see your hand in front of your face. Fall of the year it was, and everything was paper dry. Old Man Hargraves lost his shirt on that one."

"That's not what I heard," Mr. Thripp said. "I heard he got rich off the insurance."

"Him and his wife left town soon after," someone said.

"Whatever happened to them?" asked Doc Hooper.

"They got salvation and went on the road preachin' the gospel. My wife's sister run into him over in Mount Pleasant where they was havin' a tent revival. Old Hargraves said he made more money in a month spreadin' the word of God than he had in a full year ginnin' cotton."

"Do tell," the doc said. "Say, would you look at those sparks rising up. Reminds me of the Fourth of July."

Biggie had wandered over to the rope that was supposed to keep people from getting in the way. Me and Monica followed.

"Where's Rosebud?" I asked.

"Gone to help the firemen," Biggie said, never taking her eyes off the blaze. "Get that hose around back," she shouted to Fire Chief Reynolds. "It's about to set fire to that grove of chinaberry trees." The fireman next to him looked around and waved two fingers at us. He was all covered with soot, and his fireman's coat was too big for him. "Hey, J.R. Hey, Miss Biggie," he called.

I heard Fire Chief Reynolds behind him call out, "Butch, would you mind pointin' that hose at the fire. We ain't here to water the lawn, you know."

I heard a voice behind me.

"Tho thad. What a catathrophe. There goeth our mutheum."

I looked around and there stood Miss Lonie and Miss Julia. Miss Julia was scribbling away on the pad she always carries with her. The fire was reflected in their wide-open eyes, and neither of them looked one bit sad. Just excited.

"Can I quote you on that, Lonie?" Miss Julia asked.

"Of courth. Jutht thpell my name right. Latht time you . . ."

Biggie turned to Miss Julia. "How did it start?" she asked.

"Chief says they won't know for a couple of days," Miss Julia said. "Gotta let it cool down, don'cha know."

"Arson, if you ask me," said Mr. Thripp, walking up from behind a pickup truck. "Fire like that just don't start by itself."

"Norman," Biggie said, "go back to your tearoom and make up a big urn of coffee. Bring it over here for the firefighters. Get an ice chest and bring along some cold drinks, too."

"Well, I was planning—" he said.

"Get going, Norman," Miss Julia said. "I declare!"

He left, looking back over his shoulder like a dog that's being sent out in the rain.

"Biggie," I said, "can me and Monica go around back? I want to see if the fire's getting over on Mr. Oterwald's mama's place."

"Okay," Biggie said, "but I want you two to stay out of the way of the firemen. Just stand back and watch."

"Come on," Monica said, already running toward the west side that faces the vacant lot where they were planning to build the living history farm.

All the others were standing around the parking lot, so

we sat down on a big rock and watched the show all by ourselves.

Monica grabbed my arm. "J.R.," she said, pointing toward the big double doors on the back of the building that open onto the loading platform. "I saw something move in there!"

"Uh-huh," I said, still watching the sparks fly up in the dark sky.

"J.R.! Look!"

I looked, and just as I did I saw a black figure dart out the door, leap off the platform, and run toward the grove of chinaberry trees dragging a trail of wispy smoke behind it. As the creature passed through the glare of the fire, plumb buck naked, and disappeared into the trees, I heard a scream like nothing I'd ever heard before. Not human but not animal, either. Right at that moment, the roof fell in and sparks started flying everywhere. Monica and I ran to get out of the way and, in all the excitement, I forgot to tell Biggie about the burning person until the next morning at breakfast.

"It wasn't big enough to be the Wooten Creek monster," Monica said.

"I never thought it was," Biggie said. "Probably some poor soul thinking to get a good night's sleep out of the cold. More than likely he's the one that set the fire. By accident, I expect."

"What you going to do, Biggie?" I asked.

Biggie was sitting at her dresser rubbing Jergens lotion on her face and arms. She didn't say anything, just screwed the cap on the bottle and put it in a drawer. Then she took out her brush, hit her hair about three licks with it, and said, "There, I'm ready to face the day."

"Biggieee!" I said.

"Don't whine. What?"

"What are you gonna do about the person?"

"I'm going to call down to the courthouse and hand it over to the sheriff. That poor creature could be dead or dying out there somewhere."

"Run 'way out," Rosebud said the next Tuesday afternoon. "I'm gonna throw you a long one."

I ran clear over to Mrs. Moody's fence and turned to catch the football, but, as it turned out, it hit me right upside the head. I'd seen something that made me forget the ball was coming.

"What's wrong with you, boy?" Rosebud said, "That was a perfect—well, what do you know?"

The Job's Crossing fire truck had pulled up right in front of our house, and Chief Reynolds and Butch were headed for our front door.

"Is Miss Biggie here?" Butch asked. "We're here on some mighty important official business. And it-is-so-sad!"

I ran to the front door. "Bigieee!" I yelled.

"What's the news?" Biggie asked when they were all seated in the parlor.

Butch took a lace-trimmed hankie out of his pocket and dabbed at his eyes. "I just don't think I can tell it. Chief . . ."

"Well, it's this away," the chief said. "We had a little rain shower last night. That cooled down the ashes over at the depot."

"There's not any depot anymore," Butch said, sobbing into his handkerchief. "It's nothing but a stinky old pile of ashes. Oh, Chief, tell them the rest!"

"I will if you'll let me," the chief said.

Just then Willie Mae came in with a tray holding a pot of coffee and four mugs and set it down on the coffee table in front of Biggie.

"Good," Biggie said. "I always think better over a good

cup of coffee. Only thing is, I don't yet know what I'm supposed to be thinking about."

"Could I have honey instead of sugar?" Butch asked. "Ruby Muckleroy says refined sugar is very bad for your skin."

Willie Mae humphed back toward the kitchen and came back carrying the honey jar with an iced-tea spoon sticking out the top. She slammed it down in front of Butch. "Don't spill none," she said.

Butch put his hanky back into his pocket. "I won't. I promise," he said and tilted the jar, scraping half of the honey into his mug.

The chief continued like he'd never been interrupted. "So I got together a crew of volunteer firemen, and we went on over to investigate the cause of the fire." He took a sip of coffee. "Mighty good coffee, Miss Biggie," he said. "What kind do you use?"

"Something Willie Mae orders from Louisiana. Community, I think it is," Biggie said. "Now, go on. What did you find?"

"Well'm, some of the boys thought it might of started from them new heaters you had put in there, but Ike Sloan said not on your life on account of his heater man was the best in northeast Texas and had even installed the heat in the new courthouse they built over in Daingerfield."

"Tell um what Mr. Plumley thought," Butch said.

"Oh, yeah," the chief said. "Plumley thought it was spontaneous combustion from the paint rags old Peoples had been using to paint the telegraph room."

"That was water-based paint," Biggie said. "What else?"

"So I commenced poking around in the storage building, and what should I find but a big five-gallon can of diesel fuel. I reckon I should say it used to be full of diesel. It was plumb empty time I come across it."

"But that ain't all," Butch said. "Oh, no. That ain't all by a long shot."

"Whose tellin' this?" the chief said.

"Well, you, but—"

"Go on, chief," Biggie said.

"Well, I commenced poking around in them ashes and it appeared to me that that there diesel had been poured all over the place in that depot. I mean, you could see where it had burned black lines around what was left of the floor."

"So you think it was arson?" Biggie said.

"Not a doubt in the world," the chief said. "Somebody done deliberately set our depot afire on purpose!"

"But that ain't all," Butch said.

"I declare, Butch, you sound like a broken record. So what else did you find?"

"Lemme tell it," Butch said. "I found her."

"Okay. Shoot," the chief said.

"It was a body in there, Miss Biggie. A dead one," Butch said.

"You said *her*, Butch. Have you identified the body?"

"We knew it was a lady," Butch continued, ignoring Biggie's question, "because it had ladies' earrings on. Well, don't nobody but me and the ladies wear earrings in this town, and here I set, alive and kicking."

"Where's the body now?" Biggie asked.

"Doc Hooper had it taken over to the funeral home even though we ain't got a undertaker at this time. We need for you to tell us what to do next, Miss Biggie."

"Did you notify the ranger?" Biggie asked.

"No'm. Never thought of that. We come here first."

"Ranger's not available," Butch said. "He's gone to a rangers' retreat over at Lake Sam Rayburn. And that there DPS feller's just had his wisdom teeth extracted. He says he's had so much codeine he can't even remember his own name." The chief drained the last of his coffee. "Looks like you'll just have to take charge, Miss Biggie."

"Well," Biggie said, "the first thing we'll have to do is identify the corpse."

Butch pulled out his lace hankie and blew his nose real loud. "Oh, no, Miss Biggie," he said. "We don't have to do that. Nosiree. We already know who it is."

Biggie stood up. "Well, great honk, Butch! Who was it?"

Butch wasn't ready to give up having Biggie's full attention. "You see," he said, "them earrings wasn't just ordinary ladies' earrings like you'd buy at Kmart or somewhere. They was right nice earrings, ten-karat gold plated. In fact, I was with her when she bought them. It was at one of them jewelry parties Miss Crews was givin' back last summer."

Biggie sat back down.

"She quit doin' it after a couple of months. Said she'd done sold to everybody in town and she'd used up all the ladies that would agree to give another party for her . . ."

"Butch," Biggie said, "if you don't tell me who it was, I'm going to skin your head."

Butch knew when to quit.

"Why, Miss Itha, of course. She was the only one in town who'd bought that particular style."

"Oh no!" Biggie said. "Poor Itha."

Butch started blubbering into his hankie again. "It's just so sad," he said. "I can't quit thinking about how happy she looked strolling in the park holding hands with Monk the night before he died."

"What?" Biggie said.

"They was just so sweet," Butch said. "It looked to me like Little DeWayne was gonna have his daddy back."

"Butch," Biggie said, "why in the ever lovin', blue-eyed world didn't you tell me this before?"

159

Butch hung his head. "I must of forgot," he said. "After all, it ain't easy bein' acting police chief with so much crime goin' on."

"Okay," Biggie said. "You two can go now. I've got some thinking to do. This puts a whole new slant on things."

21

Miss Biggie," Willie Mae said, "what you gonna have for Thanksgiving dinner? It ain't more'n two weeks away."

"I don't know," Biggie said. "You think of something."

Willie Mae poured coffee in Biggie's cup just as the back door slammed and Rosebud came into the kitchen.

"Is that fresh coffee?" he asked.

Willie Mae just looked at him and took another mug out of the cabinet. As she poured, she said, "Not as fresh as you." She looked hard at Biggie. "Miss Biggie," she said, "you look lower than a snake's belly in a wagon track. What's ailin' you?"

"Nothing," Biggie said, sipping her coffee.

"I know what it is," I said. "Biggie's worried on account of she ain't solved old Monk's murder yet."

"It's poor Itha," Biggie said. "It's awful for anyone to have to die like that. And I guess you might be right, J.R., about the murder, I mean. Nothing seems to fit." She stirred two spoons of sugar into her coffee. "Here we are with two bodies on our hands and a case of arson, and I'm no closer to the truth than I was when we just had one corpse to worry about."

"How about that reverend?" Rosebud said. "He's got more lies than a dog's got fleas. Honey, you got any of that custard pie left?"

"Can I have some pie, too?" I asked.

Willie Mae cut pie for me and Rosebud and set it in front of us. She looked at Biggie, who shook her head. "So how come them two come here to Job's Crossing?" Willie Mae asked. "They must of had a reason."

"Dern tootin' they had a reason," Rosebud said. "And our boy here found that reason and brought it right home to his Biggie."

"The money!" I said. "But how'd they know about it?"

"I'm gettin' to that ain't I?" Rosebud said. "'Member Miss Biggie sent me to Eureka Springs on my detectin' trip? Well, in makin' a few inquiries of the locals up there, I found out that his name ain't Poteet at all. It's Parker. That mean anything to you?"

"Naw."

"Oh, J.R.," Biggie said, "don't you remember whose name was in that purse? It was Ma Parker, the bank robber. She was the reverend's daddy's sister-in-law." She reached across the table and cut herself a piece of pie. "Reach me a plate and fork, will you, Willie Mae?"

I was beginning to catch on. "So, they must of got to talking," I said, "and Monk told the rev about havin' a wife and kid here—"

"And how he might like to look in on them," Rosebud said.

"So they pooled their money to make a down payment on the funeral home, and the reverend sweet-talked the bishop into sending him here, which wasn't hard to do because,

162

much as I hate to admit it, not many strangers want to settle in a place like this," Biggie said.

"Just so they could get that money," I said. "So there it is, Biggie."

"Maybe that there reverend hadn't figured on Monk gettin' back with Miss Itha," Rosebud said. "So he up and killed Monk *and* her so he could keep the money all to himself."

"How?" Biggie asked. "That reverend's just a little squirt. He might have figured a way to burn the depot, but how would he get Itha down there? And who was that running away that night? Most important, how could he have broken every rib in Monk's body?"

"The Wooten Creek monster could," I said.

"J.R., how many times have I told you . . . Wait a minute! How could I have been so stupid? Come on, J.R., we've got to go to see that ranger."

We found the ranger sitting at the counter at the Owl Cafe drinking a cup of coffee.

Biggie told him to bring his coffee and join us at a corner booth.

First she filled his ear with all the stuff Rosebud had found out in Arkansas.

"That's an interesting mess of facts, Miss Biggie," the ranger said, "but you're going to have to throw a little more kindlin' on the fire. I don't hardly see where that gets us anywhere."

"Popolus!" Biggie yelled. "Bring me a glass of ice water. I need to oil my pipes so I can get through to this thick-headed lawman."

The ranger grinned. "I'm tryin', Miss Biggie."

Biggie talked real slow. "It doesn't get us anywhere by itself," she said. "But it does point to the fact that we've forgotton two things. First, let me ask you a question. Did your people ever find that poor thing that ran out of the depot on the night of the fire?"

"Not a trace," the ranger said. "We combed the place for a good mile all around. We couldn't even find a trail."

He looked at me like he thought me and Monica had been seein' things.

"If J.R. says he saw it, he saw it," Biggie said. "The second thing is this: Where is DeWayne? Vida says she called her aunt in Broken Bow, and her aunt said Itha and DeWayne had never even been in Broken Bow. Vida's about to go crazy grieving for Itha and worrying about DeWayne. Of course, Vida may know more than she's telling. She'd say anything Itha told her to," Biggie went on. "The woman never had a thought in her life that Itha didn't tell her to think."

"How about I bring the reverend in and question him?" the ranger asked.

"No, because he's the only tenor we've got, and I'm not about to get his hackles up before play night."

"And when is that?"

"Wednesday, the day before Thanksgiving. After that, you can grill him all you want. But I intend to have this murder solved before then."

"I guess we can wait that long," the ranger said. "But, Miss Biggie, I still don't get your drift. Just what do you want me to do?"

Biggie drained her water glass, then picked out a piece of ice with her fingers and popped it in her mouth. As soon as she'd chewed it up and swallowed it, she said, "I want you to organize a search party. I want that whole area across the creek searched. I want to know who's making those big footprints all over the place. Whoever it is may be trying to make us think the Wooten Creek monster had something to do with Monk's murder. Sure as shooting there's a human being behind all this."

"I gotta agree with you there," he said. "It might take me a day or two to organize a search party."

"Tomorrow night," Biggie said. "It's a full moon. Get plenty of help. You're going to need it."

"Right," the ranger said. "We'll give you a report the first chance we get."

"Hmm," Biggie said. "Come on, J.R. I think we'll be calling on Vida. She's bound to be needing a friend about now."

Biggie was wrong. When we got to Miss Vida's little house on Pine Avenue, we saw cars parked all up and down the street. The house was plumb full of folks that had come over to offer sympathy. I don't think I ever saw so much food in one place except at covered-dish suppers. Cakes and casseroles and salads covered the dining table and all the counter space in the kitchen. Miss Vida was sitting in her big chair eating a piece of cake and blubbering into a hanky.

"Oh, Miss Biggie," she wailed, holding out her arms to be hugged, "what am I gonna do without my baby sister? Oh, Lordy, what will I do?"

Biggie ignored her stretched-out arms and took a chair beside her, patting her knee. She looked hard into Miss Vida's eyes. "Vida," she said, "where's DeWayne?"

That caused Miss Vida to let out another scream. Chocolate icing oozed out of the corners of her mouth. "I don't know!" she shouted. "I've lost um both. I'm all alone in the world."

"No, you're not," Biggie said. "DeWayne's somewhere. We just have to find him. If he's not with your aunt in Broken Bow, could Itha have left him with any of your other relatives?"

Miss Vida let out a howl like a calf calling for its mama. "I cain't talk no more," she said. "I gotta go lay down."

Miss Lonie and Miss Mattie took her back to her bedroom, and we heard the bed springs holler as she lay down.

"It's a doggone shame," Miss Crews said. "What's that poor old thing going to do?"

Mrs. Muckleroy said one thing was for sure, she couldn't stay in the beauty business. Miss Lonie, who had come back in the room, thought she might do well as a house maid, but Mr. Thripp said she'd do better to take up farm labor.

"Working on a hay truck might sweat a few pounds off her," he said.

"We have to go," Biggie said. "We'll discuss what's to be done about Vida at the next Daughters' meeting."

Willie Mae had made chicken and dumplings for lunch, with Mexican cornbread which, if you've never had it, you've missed a lot. It's just plumb full of cheese and corn and picante sauce. I was on my second helping when I thought of something.

"Biggie," I said, "why did you want that ranger to search across the creek?"

"Because that's where we're going to be looking," she said, "and I want backup in case there's trouble."

"Why didn't you just tell him that?" Out of the corner of my eye, I saw Willie Mae pull a peach cobbler out of the oven. "Oh, boy, can we have ice cream on top?"

"Your mind jumps around like a hop-toad when there's food around," Willie Mae said. " 'Course we gonna have ice cream. Don't we always?"

"I didn't tell the ranger," Biggie said, "because he'd have had a wall-eyed fit and told us we couldn't come. Besides, I don't want a bunch of men holding us back. I think I know where DeWayne is—and probably the singed man as well."

That night, after Willie Mae and Biggie had watched their favorite TV show, Willie Mae said, "Miss Biggie, can we talk about Thanksgiving now?"

"Sure, why not?" Biggie said. "Let's see, I've invited Butch, Lonie, Julia, and the Sontags. The Sontags said they couldn't come because Coye wanted to go hunting and Ernestine's down in her back. That makes six of us."

"Biggie," I said, "can Monica come?"

"Sure," Biggie said. "You and Rosebud can go pick her up."

"Miss Biggie," Willie Mae said, "what you want to have?"

"Not turkey, Biggie. Puleese. I hate turkey!"

"How about I cook a big old fresh ham with sweet potatoes and mashed rutabagas?" Willie Mae asked.

"Urp!" I said.

"I know," Biggie said. "We'll get some Cornish game hens. Then we can have stuffing and all the trimmings."

"Boring," I said.

Rosebud spoke up. "Honey," he said, " 'member that time when you cooked that standin' rib roast with Yorkshire puddin' and English peas, candied carrots, and roasted potatoes? Um-um, that was good eatin'."

"English trifle for dessert?" Willie Mae asked.

"Perfect," Biggie said. "Maybe I'll invite Mattie and Norman, too. They need a lesson on what fine cooking is all about."

I didn't know what all that stuff was, but it had to be better than turkey, so I kept quiet.

"We'd better all turn in early," Biggie said. "We may not get any sleep at all tomorrow night."

22

Me and Rosebud were just finishing breakfast when Biggie walked into the kitchen carrying the biggest gun I'd ever seen.

"Rosebud," she said, "I want you to clean Grandpa Wooten's shotgun and then go down to Bertram Handy's and pick up a box of shells for it."

Rosebud examined the gun. "This gun's mighty old, Miss Biggie," he said. "I don't reckon Mr. Handy still carries shells to fit this thing."

"Here's Grandpa's gun-cleaning kit," Biggie said, handing him an old tin box. "You just clean the gun. I'll get the shells."

"Who you plannin' on shootin'?" Rosebud asked.

"The Wooten Creek monster, I bet," I said.

Biggie just looked at me, then back at Rosebud. "I plan on using it to call the ranger and his men if we run into trouble," she said. "That old blunderbuss will scare the squirrels out of the trees. Now, you get to cleaning while I run downtown to the hardware store."

"Can I go?" I asked.

"Nope. Not this time. I want you to go up to the attic and dig our hunting clothes out of that old wooden footlocker. Hang them out on the clothesline to air the mustiness out of them."

They were musty all right, and chewed up in places on account of a family of mice had built a nest in that footlocker.

"Gimme them," Willie Mae said when I showed her. "I'm gonna wash um up before you hang um out."

It was near noon when Biggie got back with the shells.

"I declare," she said, "that Bertram Handy's got everything from horse collars to slop jars in the back room of that store. He could open up an antique shop and make a killing. The shells were stuffed in the bottom of an old pickle barrel. He told me he hadn't thrown a thing away since his granddaddy owned the store."

"Lucky for us," Rosebud said, peering down the barrel of the gun. "Puts me in mind of the time I went huntin' with old Huey Long and his bunch. 'Course, I was just a youngun then. They taken me along to pick up the birds on account of Huey's bird dog come down with the runnys from eatin' crawfish shells—"

"Rosebud, you wasn't even a gleam in your daddy's eyeballs when that there Huey got himself shot," Willie Mae said.

Rosebud just grinned and ducked his head. "Maybe it was his brother, old Earl," he said.

"Where'd he get the crawfish shells?" I asked.

"I'll tell you later when there ain't so much negative thinkin' around," he said. "Negative thinkin' interferes with my recollections."

"You mean your lies," Willie Mae said. "Now, get that gun mess off the table so I can set out lunch."

Biggie made us all take a nap after lunch so we could stay up all night if we had to. I played with my rats and read comic books all afternoon 'til Biggie said I could come out. As it happened, I ran into too much excitement to get sleepy. Sleep was the last thing on any of our minds that night. Truth is, we were too busy trying to stay alive.

By nine o'clock, we'd dressed in our hunting gear and were on our way to the creek.

"Did you bring the flashlight?" Biggie asked Rosebud.

"Miss Biggie, what do you think I am? You think I'm dumb enough to go out in them woods without no light?"

"I got mine, too," I said.

"Did you bring the gun and shells?"

"Yes'm. Brought them, too."

I had a feeling Biggie was nervous, which made my belly ball up into a knot. It takes a heap to rattle Biggie.

"Go down to the low-water crossing and drive across," Biggie said as we caught sight of the creek.

"I don't know... in this car—" Rosebud said.

"Rosebud, we can make it. It hasn't rained in a month. More than likely it's dry as Moses crossing the Red Sea."

Biggie was right. We drove across on dry sand and gravel. Rosebud parked the car in the same clearing where we'd had our camp-out.

"Let me see," Biggie said, "it's been a long time, but I think it's down this way."

She started off down the Cherokee Trace, and we followed.

"What, Biggie? Where are we going?" I asked.

"Why, to Cooter's cabin, of course," she said.

I was shining my light on the ground, looking for monster tracks, but didn't see a one. "That's right peculiar," I said.

"What, son?" Rosebud asked.

"No monster tracks," I said. "Remember, Rosebud, when we was out here, they were all over the place?"

"Good," Biggie said. "That confirms my theory. Now turn here and head through that grove of pines. If you look real good, you'll see an old cattle path."

When we got in under those pine trees, it got real spooky on account of we didn't have the moonlight to see by. Suddenly, I heard something. It was crashing through the bushes to the right of us, and it was big.

Rosebud stopped. "Y'all hear that?" he whispered.

We all stopped and listened, but whatever it was had stopped, too. The woods were so quiet you could hear a worm sneeze.

"Must have been a cow," Biggie said.

"More'n likely," Rosebud said.

I shivered.

I was puffing and blowing when we finally came to a clearing that was lit up with moonlight. In the middle of the clearing was the sorriest excuse for a house I'd ever seen. It seemed to be built out of packing crates and rusty tin and used lumber scrounged up from who knows where. It had an old tin stovepipe sticking out the roof with smoke coming out the top. A dim light shone through the one dirty window.

"Yep. This is it," Biggie said, stepping up on the rickety front stoop. She knocked on the door.

When the door opened, I jumped off that porch and started running back toward the woods. Rosebud caught me and drug me back. What I saw standing in that door was scarier than Freddie, scarier that Frankenstein, scarier than anything I'd ever seen in my life. Its head and face were fiery red except where the blisters were, and in places the skin was peeling, leaving snow-white skin underneath. It was bald as an egg.

"Why, Miss Biggie," it said, "y'all come on in. I was just cookin' up some side meat and grits. Y'all want some?"

"No thanks, Cooter," Biggie said. "We just came to ask you some questions—but now I see you need medical attention. Why don't we drive you back to town to the hospital?"

"Shoot, Miss Biggie, I'm okay," Cooter said. " 'Scuse me, I gotta turn my meat."

He turned the meat over and then, I guess, decided it was done, because he dished it up on a cracked plate and heaped a big pile of grits beside it. He pulled a wooden box over to a cable spool he was using for a table and started in eating. "Y'all can set on my bed, if you've a mind to," he said.

We sat down in a row on the old army cot he used for a bed. It was dirty and stinky, and I was glad we'd worn our hunting suits over our other clothes. Then I noticed something. The bed was covered with Uncle Carbuncle Wooten's buffalo robe. I didn't say anything right then because Biggie had already started in asking Cooter questions.

"Cooter," she said, "what happened down at the depot?"

"It was all Miss Itha's idea," he said. "You ain't gonna get me in trouble, are you?"

"Not if I can help it," Biggie said. "Why did Itha want to burn the depot?"

Cooter sopped up the grease on his plate with a piece of white bread and crammed it in his mouth.

"Well, you see, it went like this here," he said. "She wanted to get that money—you know, the money that was hid out back somewheres."

"How did she know it was there?"

172

"On account of that preacher man, don'cha know. He'd done told old Monk and Monk told Miss Itha."

"But why burn the depot?"

"On account of, don'cha see, everybody in town ud be watching the fire and us two could sneak out back and grab the money without bein' noticed. Leastways that's the way Miss Itha had it figured."

"Itha never was too bright," Biggie said. "Now—"

Cooter shook his head. "Miss Biggie," he said, "you know I'm just a poor old ignorant feller that ain't hardly got a way to make a livin' . . ."

Biggie reached in her pocket and pulled out a twenty-dollar bill. "That make it any easier?" she asked.

Cooter looked at the bill like he'd never seen such a thing in his life. "Lordy mercy," he said. "Is that one of them twenties?"

"Yep," Biggie said. "Now, how did you get involved with Itha and her scheme?"

"First, let me put my brand-new twenty in my wallet," Cooter said. "Oops, I done forgot, I lost the thing. Anyway, Miss Itha needed a place to stay where nobody'd even think about lookin' for her. After Monk got killed, she planned on outsmartin' that preacher and keepin' the money for herself."

"So she never went to Broken Bow?"

"What's that?"

"A town in Oklahoma where Itha was supposed to be gone to."

"Well, no'm. Not that I know of. Her and the kid stayed here the whole time. See that old army tent outside?" He pointed toward the back window. "They slept back there. Before Miss Itha g-got . . ."

Cooter started in blubbering and couldn't talk for a whole minute.

173

Biggie patted him on the shoulder. "I'm sorry, Cooter," she said.

"Yes'm, I was right fond of her," Cooter said, wiping his eyes on an old dirty dishrag.

I got up and started walking around the cabin. In the corner behind some old boxes I saw something real strange. It was a pair of stilts, tall ones, and tied on the bottom of them were Aunt Vida's old clown shoes that she gave to Goodwill. I picked one up and brought it back to Biggie.

"Well, bless Pat," Biggie said, "it looks like you've found your Wooten Creek monster. I expect the rest of his costume was Uncle Carbuncle's buffalo robe, which we're sitting on right now. What have you got to say about this, Cooter?"

"You're right, ma'am," Cooter said. "At first I was just prankin' around with um, but Miss Itha, she said it ud be a good way to keep folks away from here, so then I just made them tracks all over the place. Shore scared you and your little friend girl on y'all's camp-out, didn't I?" he said to me with a big old toothless grin.

I didn't say a word. I was plenty mad at being tricked like that.

"So was it you outside Monk's window the night he was killed?" Biggie asked.

"Sho," Cooter said.

"What did you see?" she asked.

"Well, now, Miss Biggie, twenty bucks is a powerful lot of money, but I reckon that there's right valuable information. You reckon you could . . . ?"

"Nope," Biggie said. "I already have a pretty good idea who did Monk in—and if we need to, we can subpoena you and make you tell."

"Well'm, okay," Cooter said. "What else y'all need to know?"

"Just a couple of things," Biggie said. "How did you get

174

away from the depot without leaving any trail? The lawmen tried to track you."

Cooter giggled. "Hee-hee-hee. I knowed they was chasin' me, but I didn't care. I headed for that branch that runs just across the tracks, past them chinaberry trees, and jumped right in. I just lay there in that cool water 'til I could get the strength to come on back home. Then, I just follered the branch 'til it run into Wooten Creek. Is that all, Miss Biggie? I'm gettin' right tired of talkin'."

"Just one more question," Biggie said. "Where is De-Wayne?"

"Oh, him. I taken him over to Betty Jo Darling's place. It ain't far from here. Want me to show you?"

"I know where it is," Biggie said, standing up. "I'll send you out some food and medicine for those burns tomorrow—and pick up my uncle's buffalo rug." She started for the door. "Come on, you two," she said, "it's quite a little trek to Betty Jo's place."

"Wait a minute, Biggie," I said. "I gotta ask Cooter something."

"Okay, but hurry."

"Did your wallet have a picture of a four-foot grasshopper in it?"

"Sho," Cooter said, "and some right valuable coupons, too."

I ran to catch up with Biggie and Rosebud, who were walking away. When I caught up, I told Biggie about finding Cooter's wallet.

"I'll look at it when we get home," she said. "Right now we've got other fish to fry."

23

Biggie led us back to the Cherokee Trace. This time we headed in the opposite direction from Cooter's place. The trace meandered along the creek bank for, I guess, half a mile, then we came to a cow pasture surrounded by a bob-wire fence. Rosebud held the wires apart so Biggie could shinny through.

"Get down lower," he said to Biggie. "You 'bout to scratch your back."

When it was my turn, I said, "I can do it. You let go and let me show you how."

Rosebud let go of the wires and I rolled across under the bottom wire. That was a mistake; I rolled right across a fresh cow pattie.

"Now you done decorated yourself up good," Rosebud said. "Pee-yew! Walk downwind of us."

I didn't have time to feel stupid because I could feel hoof-beats shaking the ground right behind me. I looked around and saw the biggest Brahma bull in the whole world, and he looked mad as a cornered cottonmouth.

"Run!" Biggie yelled, and we skittered across that pasture just ahead of that bull. I could feel his breath on my neck.

I don't remember how we got to the other side, or how we got across the opposite fence. I just remember standing there shaking and panting while that bull snorted and tossed his head at us from inside that pasture.

When I could talk, I said, "Biggie, how we gonna get back to the car?"

"Never mind," she said, "this was just a shortcut. We'll go back the long way."

"How much further, Miss Biggie?" Rosebud asked.

"Just beyond those woods," Biggie answered. "Not more than a mile."

I opened my mouth to complain, but realized that it would be useless as an outhouse on a submarine, so I just took off toward those woods ahead of the others. Just as I got about ten yards into the trees, I heard something crashing through the woods just like the last time. I shinnied up a dogwood tree. Cooter or no Cooter, I knew there wasn't nothing but the Wooten Creek monster that could make that much racket.

I was peering around to see if I could see him when Biggie and Rosebud caught up with me. "Get down out of that tree and come on," Biggie said. "Good grief. We'll never get there."

I tried to tell Biggie what I'd heard, but she just tramped on, not paying me any mind.

Finally, she pointed directly in front of us. "See that light?" she said. "That's Betty Jo Darling's place."

She trotted ahead, and by the time me and Rosebud caught up, she was knocking on the door of a little square sharecropper's cabin. The door opened just a crack, and Betty Jo stared out at us. She'd probably still be staring if Biggie hadn't spoke up.

"It's me, Betty Jo. Biggie Weatherford. Can we come in?"

Betty Jo might have been smiling as she opened the door and stood aside for us. I couldn't tell for sure on account of her buck teeth.

"J.R. you pull off your hunting suit before you come in," Biggie said.

When I finally got a look inside, I was surprised. This place wasn't a thing like Cooter's. Although it was just one room, it was pretty near the cleanest place I'd ever seen. The old wore-out linoleum was waxed and shiny, the plates were lined up on a shelf over a table next to the window, and the table held a blue pitcher full of dried flowers. The wash table that held the dishpan and a bucket of well water had a little ruffeldy skirt around it. Three beds were lined up on the opposite wall and were covered with patchwork quilts. A shiny black-iron stove set in the middle of the room and sitting on the floor in front of it were the two Darling kids and DeWayne playing Monopoly.

DeWayne looked up at me. "Hey, J.R.," he said. "Did you miss me? I been stayin' out here on account of my mama got burnt up in a fire. Did you hear about that?"

"Yeah," I said.

"Old Cooter got burnt, too," DeWayne said.

"Yeah, I know," I said.

The other kids had scooted up against the wall and were staring at Rosebud, who was standing by the door holding his shotgun. He grinned at them, showing his gold hearts and clubs and spades and diamonds. They scuddled across the room and crawled under the table.

Biggie and Betty Jo had sat themselves on one of the beds and were having a conversation.

178

"How's Aunt Vida?" DeWayne asked.

"Not too good," I said. "I reckon we came to take you home."

"Well, I ain't goin'," DeWayne said. "I like it here."

"Okay," I said, and squatted down by the Monopoly board. "Who's winning?"

"Me," DeWayne said. "Franklin and Angie Jo ain't very good at games, but they can sure climb trees and track armadillos."

"Why would they want to do that? Track armadillos, I mean."

DeWayne looked at me like I had all the brains of a bowling ball. "To eat, of course," he said.

"Y'all eat armadillos?"

"Sure, and squirrels and lots of fish," he said. "Betty Jo's a mighty good cook."

I glanced over toward the bed and saw that Betty Jo was grinning over her buck teeth like she could swallow a banana sideways. Then I heard a sound. Rosebud heard it, too, because he swung his head around and started toward the door. Before he got there, it burst open.

And there it was. The Wooten Creek monster. It had wild red hair that stuck out all over its head and was full of briars and leaves. It was covered in an old army blanket with holes cut out for arms. Its face, all smeared with dirt, had the meanest look I'd ever seen anywhere—and it was carrying a shotgun almost as big as Grandpa Wooten's.

Then it spoke. "I want my baby," it said, and I knew it was only Miss Vida.

DeWayne crawled under the table with the other kids. I saw Rosebud ease behind Miss Vida and out the door. Biggie and Betty Jo just sat on the bed and stared their eyes out. As usual, Biggie rose to the occasion.

"Why, Vida," she said, "what in Sam Hill are you doing 'way out here?"

"I come for my baby," Miss Vida growled, "and I'll shoot ever'body in the place if I have to."

Boom.

I looked down at to see if I'd been shot, then realized that it must of been Rosebud shooting outside to call the lawmen. I didn't have much hope of them coming on account of we hadn't seen hide nor hair of them all that night, but I sure hoped they would.

Biggie spoke up, real slow and soft. "Come on over here and sit down, Vida," she said. "Pull that old blanket off. Betty Jo here was just about to make us some coffee."

"Hain't mot na bofe," Betty Jo said. "Mot asafrs bee."

"Good," Biggie said. "I declare, I haven't had sassafras tea in I can't remember when. How about you, Vida?"

Biggie poked Betty Jo, who got up and filled the kettle and set it on the stove.

Miss Vida bent over and looked under the table. "Get your stuff, baby, we're goin' home," she said.

DeWayne stuck out his tongue at her. "Ain't goin'," he said.

Miss Vida threw back her head and howled like a bluetick hound, then looked at Betty Jo with crazy eyes. "What have you done to my baby?" she said in a voice that sounded like she was possessed by a demon. She moved toward Betty Jo and, just as she did, an arm reached through the door and grabbed the shotgun out of her hand. Rosebud stepped in and pointed the gun at her.

"Now you go set down like Miss Biggie told you to," he said.

Miss Vida sagged like all the air had gone out of her and

plopped down on the floor. She put her face in her hands and started bawling her head off. I almost felt sorry for her.

Betty Jo put some sassafras roots in the kettle and took it off the fire. Next, she took down four mugs and poured the tea in them. She didn't say nothing, just handed one to Miss Vida and nodded to Biggie and Rosebud to come get their own. I went and stood beside Rosebud, waiting to see what was going to happen next. Nobody said a word, just sipped their tea while Miss Vida sniffed and blubbered.

I didn't have long to wait. Suddenly, the door burst open and the ranger, Trooper John Wayne Odle, and Butch rushed in, all pointing guns. Butch's was a little silver pistol he used to hold down the papers on his desk. I doubted if it had ever been fired.

"Everybody up against the wall! Oh—" John Wayne said.

"Holster your guns, boys," Biggie said.

Butch walked over and looked at Miss Vida. "Is that the Wooten Creek monster?" he asked.

"I ain't no monster, you little peckerwood," Miss Vida said.

"Good," Butch said. "Is that you, Vida?"

Miss Vida just grunted. "I'm hungry," she said.

Betty Jo got a biscuit off a pan on the back of the stove and handed it to her and watched her eat it in two bites.

"What's going on here, Miss Biggie?" the ranger asked.

"I'll tell you all about it tomorrow," Biggie said. "In the meantime, you'd best take Vida home. Post a guard at her house. She's in no frame of mind to be running loose. And Butch, you go and find Doc Hooper. Tell him to go over and give her a shot of something. A big one."

It was after one when we got home. I'd never stayed up so late in my life except for the time me and Monica got pitched

181

into a pit and stayed there the best part of the night before Biggie and Rosebud found us.

Willie Mae had waited up for us.

"You should of been there, Willie Mae," I said. "You could have done a voodoo spell on Miss Vida. She looked like she was possessed to me." I'd just seen an old movie on TV about a little girl that had a demon in her. This priest had to do a whole lot of praying to get it out.

"You don't know nothing about possessed," Willie Mae said. "You want some of this here hot apple cider?"

"Yes'm."

We were all too excited to sleep, so we stayed up 'til two drinking cider and eating gingerbread.

I slept until eleven o'clock the next morning. When I came down for breakfast, Biggie and Rosebud were gone.

Willie Mae had a pot of stew bubbling on the stove for lunch and was just putting a pan of biscuits in the oven.

"You eat toast and jelly," she said. "I got lunch pert' near ready."

"Where'd Biggie and Rosebud go?" I asked.

"How come you gotta know everything?" Willie Mae asked.

I know how to get around Willie Mae, so I said, "Umm, this jelly's good. Is it some of your homemade?"

"Did you ever see store jelly around here?" she asked. "They went to see that ranger and then they was goin' out to that Cooter's place to fetch the smelly old buffalo robe that Miss Biggie's so partial to. I reckon they took along some food and medicine and stuff, too."

The sun was shining in through the kitchen window. "Is it cold outside?" I asked.

"Naw," Willie Mae said.

"Can I take my toast out on the front porch?"

"Want another piece? You've done ate those two I gave you?"

"Yes'm."

Me and Booger sat on the porch and waited for Biggie and Rosebud to get back. When they finally did, Biggie was grinning like a barrel of possum heads.

"What's so funny, Biggie?" I asked.

"I know who did it," she said. "I know who killed Monk."

"Who?" I asked. "How'd you find out, Biggie?"

"You'll have to wait," she said. "Everybody's going to have to wait. There'll be time enough to arrest the culprit after we get this play behind us."

24

"Biggie," I said, "why do we have to be at the auditorium at five when the play don't start until seven?"

"Doesn't," she said. "Doesn't start until seven. Because we have to get into our costumes in plenty of time for Butch to do our makeup."

"But that's just for ladies," I said. "Why do I have to go so early? I could ride my bike. . . ."

Biggie looked at me over her newspaper. "Everybody wears makeup," she said, "even the men."

I yelled. "I ain't wearin' makeup. Biggie, the whole seventh grade's gonna be there!"

"Everybody wears makeup," Biggie said again. "If you don't, you'll look like a dead person in front of the footlights."

I sat down on the hassock in front of Biggie's chair. "Biggie, I'd rather look like a dead person. I *want* to look like a dead person. I could be a British tar that got drowned. See?"

"J.R., get out of here and let me read my paper," Biggie

184

said. "Go outside and help Rosebud put out those pansies I bought from Ike Sloan."

Rosebud had dug out two new flower beds on either side of the front steps and was sticking little bitty flowers in the ground. I stood beside him and watched.

"Them little dudes will look right fine once they come up a bit," he said, "and they'll just keep on smilin' up at you even if it snows on um."

"Who cares," I said.

Rosebud looked up at me. "I care," he said. "Hey, what's eatin' on you?"

"Makeup's eatin' me," I said. "Rosebud, did you ever hear in your whole life of a man wearin' makeup?"

"Sure," Rosebud said. "Why, cher, down on Bourbon Street, there's a place where people pay good money to see fellers wearin' makeup. Not only that, but they got on women's clothes and wigs and even jewelry, some of um. Tell the truth, them guys look right pretty, too." He picked up one of the pansy plants. "Pretty as this little pansy face."

"I ain't got time for one of your stories," I said. "Rosebud, this is serious. Biggie says I have to put on makeup for that show. What am I gonna do, Rosebud?"

"That wasn't no story, son," Rosebud said, "but I do recall the time makeup saved a man's life." He moved over to the steps and sat down. "Set down here beside me, and I'll tell you about it."

I figured I had 'til five, so I sat.

"Feller's name was Claud Landry, from down around Big Mamou. Old Claud used to catch gar fish and take them down on Main Street come Saturday and sell um to the pore folks to eat. Oowee! Them old gar got as many bones as a stray dog's got fleas."

"I hate fish bones," I said.

"So did them pore folks," Rosebud said, "but they

185

couldn't afford nothin' else to eat. Well, one evenin' Claud was settin' in his boat runnin' his line out and not catchin' nothin' but a few little old mud cats." Rosebud pulled a half-smoked cigar out of his pants pocket and lit it. He took a big pull and continued. "Old Claud was gettin' right depressed, don'cha see, on account of he was mighty much in love with Terese Hebert, and Terese's papa had done tole him he couldn't marry Terese until he'd made enough money to buy her a nice little house with a gas stove and indoor plumbing."

"Rosebud," I said, "this ain't got one single thing to do with makeup."

"Hold your horses," Rosebud said. "Ain't I gettin' to that? So, anyway, Claud figured he might just as well head on back to town seein' as how them fish wasn't hungry that day. Well, just as he got his oar in the water, what did he see but a big old gater swimmin' circles around his boat.

" 'Git outta here and leave me alone,' Claude yelled.

"Well, just then that old gator swum up to the boat and stuck his head plumb outta the water.

" 'Woo-wee,' the gator said, 'I done found my supper.'

"Old Claud had to think fast. 'Wait a minute, Mr. Gator,' he said. 'Mayor Hebert's wife, Miz Jenetta, she mighty plump and tender. Juicy, too, I guarantee. If you'll wait 'til tomorrow 'bout this time, I'll have her here in this very spot, and you can feast away on 'er.'

"Old gator 'lowed as how that might be okay, long as Claud come on back the very next day. 'Course Claud had to come back. That there was the best fishin' spot in the whole bayou."

"How was he gonna get the mayor's wife out there?" I asked.

"I'm gettin' to that, ain't I?" Rosebud said. "Go in the

house and get me a cup of coffee to wet my pipes so I can continue this story.

"What old Claud done," Rosebud continued when he had his coffee, "was he plumped hisself up good with some pillows and put on a big old dress he swiped off his sister. Then he taken white flour outta his mama's biscuit bowl and painted his face up good with that. Next, he taken a coal off the fire and blackened his eyes and painted up his cheeks and lips with paprika. He put on his mama's big Sunday straw hat with the cherries on it to cover his old bald head."

Rosebud slapped his knees and laughed without making any noise. "Lordy, me, that Claud must of been a sight. Anyway, next thing he done was to swipe the pot of gumbo his mama was savin' for supper. He poured 'bout four bottles of good Louisiana hot sauce in the pot and set off for the bayou. Sure 'nuff, there was that old gator waitin' for his supper.

" 'You sure looks plump, and you sure looks tasty,' the gator said, 'and me, I'm gonna eat you right now, I guarantee.'

" 'Wait, Mr. Gator,' Claud said in a real high, squeaky voice. 'I done brought you a little appetizer. Open your mouth wide now, and I'll pour it right in—best gumbo a gator ever tasted—just full of crabmeat and shrimps and good old catfish.'

"Well, that old gator opened his mouth wide, and Claud went to shakin' when he seen them big old teeth, but he grabbed that pot of gumbo and poured it right in."

"What happened?" I asked.

"Wellsir, that old gator commenced floppin' around in the water and slappin' his tail 'til he stirred up a tidal wave in that bayou. Capsized the boat, don'cha know, and Claud fell out in the water."

"Ooo-wee, did the gator eat him?"

"Shoot no, boy. Old Claud swum like a minnow even draggin along his sister's dress and his mama's best feather pillows (his mama's Sunday hat fell off in the water) 'til he got back to shore. Eventually, Claud save up enough money sellin' gar fish to buy a nice little house so he could marry Terese. So, you see, a little makeup can be a good thing, now and then."

"I ain't wearin' makeup," I said.

Biggie had been standing at the door listening. "Get upstairs and get dressed," she said. "It's almost time to go."

As soon as Butch got through with me, I peeked through the curtains at the audience. Sure enough, the whole school was there including everybody in my class. I'd probably have to get in trouble the next day on account I knew Bo Turner was going to rag me bad about having to wear makeup and this sissy sailor suit. I'd have to fight him; no getting around it.

The ranger and John Wayne Odle had set themselves in the front row and were looking mighty official.

The high school band didn't strike up the overture until 7:15 on account of Meredith Michelle having a crying fit because she said Butch made her look like a circus clown.

Butch got mad. "It's stage makeup, you silly thing," he said, stomping his foot. "You got to put a lot on or it won't show under the lights."

By the time Mrs. Muckleroy got Meredith Michelle settled down, Mr. Thripp wanted to know if Butch could tape his ears back so they wouldn't stick out so, and Miss Julia stepped on the ruffles on the bottom of her skirt and tore them loose. While Willie Mae was sewing them back, the reverend hollered that he was telling the band director to get started and, if everybody wasn't onstage in two minutes, the play was starting without them.

It's a pretty silly play, if you ask me. There's this captain of a ship, HMS *Pinafore*, and he's got a daughter, Meredith Michelle, who's in love with a sailor, Reverend Poteet, but the captain, Rosebud, thinks his daughter is too good to marry a common sailor. He wants her to marry a Sir Joseph Porter, who thinks he's better than everybody. He's willing to marry the captain's daughter anyway on account of, I guess, she's so pretty or something. So what they do is they all stand around singing a bunch of stupid songs until Biggie, who is Little Buttercup, comes out and tells everybody she used to be a baby-sitter. What she did was she mixed up the captain and Ralph, the sailor, when they were little bitty babies. That makes Ralph better than the captain. Get it? So then they all stand around singing some more because Meredith Michelle can marry the reverend on account of he is now better than she is but doesn't care. Here's the really weird part. Little Buttercup (Biggie) is in love with Rosebud (the captain) even though he must be a whole lot younger than she is on account of she took care of him when he was a baby. So we all sing some more and it's over. I told you it was weird.

The audience must not have thought so. They clapped a lot and yelled out "Bravo!" and the cast took bows and Butch came out and handed bouquets of flowers to Biggie and Meredith Michelle.

The way I've got it figured, it don't take much to entertain the folks in Job's Crossing.

Just as they took their last bow, I heard a commotion in the back row.

"Lemme by," a voice said. "I got a bone to pick with Biggie Weatherford. Biggie, you come on out here and fight like a—like a, uh, a person!"

Biggie stopped bowing and, cupping her hand over her forehead, peered over the footlights. "Why, Vida Mae," she said. "How'd you get away? I thought Codella Weems was keeping an eye on you."

"Never mind," Miss Vida said. "I come here to fight you. Now come on down off that stage."

The ranger and John Wayne had been inching up behind her. Now they each grabbed her by an arm. She shook um off like they was nothing and crouched down like a prize-fighter with her fists up.

"Come on down here, you coward," she said.

Biggie whispered to Rosebud, who jumped over the foot-lights and snuck around behind Miss Vida. He said something to the ranger and John Wayne and the three of them rushed Miss Vida and wrestled her to the floor. In a second, the ranger had her hands cuffed behind her back.

Biggie motioned to Mr. Oterwald to draw the curtain, and the show was over.

Biggie scrambled down off the stage and stood looking down at Vida.

"Help her up," she said to Rosebud. Then she turned to Miss Vida. "Are you hurt, honey?" she asked.

Miss Vida looked like all the fight was gone out of her. "No'm," she said, not looking at Biggie.

"Rosebud," Biggie said, "I want you to take J.R. on home. I'm going with the officers to see that Vida's taken care of properly."

"But, Biggie, I'm . . ."

Biggie didn't hear me. She was already pushing through the crowd to clear a way for the police leading Miss Vida.

When Biggie finally came home, it was almost midnight. Me and Willie Mae and Rosebud were sitting by the fire in the den waiting to find out what had happened.

"Off to bed," she said to me, "and don't forget to feed those rats."

190

"One question?" I said.

"Just one."

"How come Miss Vida's mad at you?"

"That's complicated, J.R.," Biggie said. "In the first place, Vida's lost everything. The only people she ever loved were Itha and DeWayne, and now they're gone. I think her mind, what there was of it, just snapped." Biggie sighed a big old sigh. "And the sad thing is, it's not over yet."

"What, Biggie? What's not over yet?"

"You said one question," Biggie said, "and I'm not sure I know the answer to the second one. Now get to bed!"

This here's a standin' rib roast, and it cost a more'n a used washing machine. She said . . . . . . slap a sweet roll . . . . . . of the . . . . and it was a shame . . . . . .

25

Thanksgiving that year was one of those days that make you plumb glad to be alive in east Texas. Football weather, my daddy used to call it. The sky was blue as Biggie's eyes, and a few orange and red leaves still hung on the trees up and down the street. I jumped out of bed so fast it made Booger arch his back and scoot out of the room like a rocket.

I dressed and followed the smell of Willie Mae's sweet potato pies to the kitchen.

"Get up, Rosebud," I said. "We gotta go get Monica."

"Set down, boy," Rosebud said. "Willie Mae's done made us some big old cinnamon rolls with pecans sprinkled on top." He wiped the sugar off his face with his napkin while Willie Mae filled his coffee mug. "Shoot, it ain't but seven o'clock. That gal prob'ly ain't even up yet."

Willie Mae went back to the counter, where she was rubbing garlic and pepper on the biggest hunk of meat I'd ever seen. I went over and stood beside her.

"What's that?" I asked.

"This here's a standin' rib roast, and it cost enough to buy a used washing machine," she said. "Git over there and get you a sweet roll. I gotta get the seasoning just right."

"Where's Biggie?" I asked.

"Still sleepin', I reckon," Willie Mae said. "She's had a mighty tiring time here lately."

That was true. Biggie'd been real busy going places and doing things without taking me with her and then not telling anybody what she was up to.

"I'm not sleeping," Biggie said from the doorway. "Who could? With those smells coming from this kitchen, I woke myself up drooling. Um-um, I'm hungry enough to eat J.R.'s rats."

"When's dinner?" I asked.

"Two o'clock on the dot," Biggie said. "I've told our guests to arrive at one."

"Who all's comin', Miss Biggie?" Rosebud asked.

Biggie plopped down at the table and took a big swig of coffee. "Norman and Mattie," she said, "Lonie, Julia, Butch—and I've invited the ranger because he's a single gentleman who doesn't have any family to go to."

"Biggie's got a boyfriend. . . ." I sang.

Rosebud grinned into his coffee cup, but Biggie didn't say nothing, just got up and poured herself a glass of orange juice.

I watched the Thanksgiving Day parades by myself on account of Willie Mae kept Rosebud busy helping her do stuff in the kitchen. It was pretty near noon before Rosebud stuck his head in the door and said, "Shake a leg, son. We got to go pick up your little friend girl."

When we got there, we had to wait while Mrs. Sontag packed up a box full of fudge and divinity and pecan logs for us to eat in case we ran out of food.

By the time we got back home, all the guests were sitting around the living room drinking wine out of Biggie's little bitty wineglasses. The sun shone in through the lace curtains, and someone had built a fire in the fireplace. Willie Mae came out of the kitchen wearing a ruffeldy white apron and handed me and Monica a glass of ginger ale.

"I believe I'll have a Big Red," I said.

Willie Mae glared at me, and I shut up, figuring this must be another one of those social graces Biggie and Willie Mae are always trying to put off on me.

Monica took one sip of her ginger ale and made a face. "Ooh, this tastes like cat pi—" she said before I clapped my hand over her mouth.

"Now, Biggie," Miss Julia said, "the talk all up and down the street is that you solved Monk's murder. It's high time you and your ranger friend here came clean. I'm betting on that reverend, myself. That feller never did ring true to me."

"You lose, ma'am," the ranger said, "although, with all the lies he was telling, he sure had us going for a while."

"Why didn't you arrest him?" asked Mr. Thripp.

Rosebud had slipped away to watch the ball games in the den. Now he came back into the room. "Can't arrest a man for being greedy," he said. "Seems to me like the jailhouses ud be right full if you could." He looked right at Mr. Thripp, who turned red all over.

"That's right," the ranger said, "all he ever did was tell a bunch of lies to the good people of the church and try to find some money that might rightfully belong to him—if it hadn't been stolen, that is."

"So did you just let him go?" asked Miss Mattie.

The ranger grinned. "I believe Mr. Oterwald and the other members of the vestry expressed a unanimous interest in his leaving town and going back to Arkansas, where he came from," he said.

Mr. Thripp sat real tall in his chair. "As a member of the vestry myself, I can confirm that to be a fact," he said.

"That's right," Biggie said. "The bishop is sending an interim rector from the diocese in Dallas until we can find someone to take that young stump sucker's place."

"Tho who did it?" Miss Lonie asked, leaning toward Biggie.

"I'll tell," Biggie said. "But first let's go back ten years to when Itha first came to town."

"Why?" asked Mr. Thripp.

"Just shut up and listen, Norman," Miss Mattie said. "The only way we'll find out is to let Biggie tell it in her own way."

"I'd gone to town on an errand," Biggie said, "and as I was coming out of the drugstore, the bus from Texarkana pulled up, and who should get off but Itha—big as a barn and black and blue all over. I started to take her to Vida's house, but on the way she began groaning and moaning like she was going to die."

"Labor pains, I'll bet," Butch said. "I heard that really hurts."

"Yep," Biggie said. "Labor pains and bruises where that Monk Carter had beaten her like a plow mule. I turned the car around and headed straight for the hospital—called Vida from there."

"Thith thory'th taking a long time," Miss Lonie said. "I believe I'll jutht have another tiny thip of wine." She reached for the decanter on the table and filled her glass to the brim.

"Well," Biggie said, "who should be in the very next bed to Itha but Betty Jo Darling, poor thing. It was soon after Donny Joe got ground up at the brick plant. There she was, having a baby all by herself." Biggie rang a little glass bell beside her chair, and Willie Mae came, wiping her hands on a towel. The way she looked at that bell, I thought it might just bust to smithereens. Biggie asked Willie Mae to fill the decanter and pour more wine all around.

"It was a long night," Biggie continued. "Itha and Betty Jo hollered and yelled until three in the morning. Finally, both babies popped out at almost the exact same minute." Biggie grabbed a handful of nuts from a cut-glass bowl and crammed them into her mouth. She chewed real slow and washed the nuts down with a big slug of wine.

"That remindth me," Miss Lonie said, "whatht going to happen to poor little DeWayne now that Vidath gone nutty as a fruitcake?"

Biggie smiled. "That's where fate stepped in," she said. "Itha's baby was stillborn, probably from all the beatings she took from Monk. Nobody knew but old Doctor Hazel-wood—he's dead now—and Vida and me. While Itha slept, I sat by Betty Jo's bed, all night, and we talked. Betty Jo begged me to put her baby in Itha's crib because she didn't see a way she could raise it right, what with already having Angie Jo and Franklin Joe to care for. So I did it. I wasn't at all sure that the little tyke wouldn't be much better off with the twins, but it sure would ease the burden on Betty Jo."

"Biggie!" I said. "Just like in the play—you mixed those babies up."

"You're right," she said, "but I did it on purpose. And here's the good part. I've found a little house over on Cy-press Street where the rent's cheap, and Betty Jo has agreed to move to town and put the children in school. DeWayne will stay with her, of course, because—well, he's hers."

Mr. Thripp spoke up. "How's she going to live? Go on welfare and let the taxpayers support her, I suppose."

"Nope," Biggie said. "I'm sending her to beauty school in Center Point. She's going to take over the salon."

"Goody," Butch said. "Will she be through in time to do Meredith Michelle's hair for the pageant?"

Biggie nodded, looking downright pleased with herself.

"But Biggie," I said. "Who killed Monk? That's what I want to know now that we know for sure there ain't no Wooten Creek monster."

"Who do you think?" Biggie said.

Mr. Thripp thought it might have been Betty Jo on account of lately she'd been seen trying to look through the window at the beauty shop.

"Probably wanted her kid back," he said.

"Real smart, Norman," Miss Julia said. "You reckon she set fire to the depot too because she just happened to know Itha Rae was in there? After all, killing Monk wasn't gonna get DeWayne back. She'd still have Itha and Vida to deal with."

"I think it was that old dirty Cooter," Miss Mattie said. "He never was worth the powder and lead it ud take to shoot him, and he used to stare at Itha all the time, in a funny kind of way—downright nasty, I thought."

"And there's still the matter of the weapon," Miss Julia said. "What'd they kill him with? Come on, Biggie. For the love of LBJ, tell us."

"Y'all are all wrong," Monica said. "I betcha it was Miss Vida that done it. She's the only one big enough and strong enough."

Mr. Thripp sniffed. "What does a little girl know?" he asked.

Miss Julia hooted a laugh. "Child, do you mean to say that poor old dumb Vida outwitted a Texas Ranger, not to mention Biggie Weatherford? I don't believe it."

"She's right," Biggie said. "Vida killed him."

The ranger turned red all the way down to his shirt collar.

"I gotta admit," he said, "she had us stumped for a while there."

"I bet I know how she did it," I said. "I bet a hundred dollars she bashed him to pieces with that iron soldier I found."

The ranger grinned at me. "I'll take that bet," he said, "and you can pay up right now on account of the only fingerprints on that iron soldier belonged to Monk Carter, which means he was probably trying to defend himself with it."

Mr. Thripp kept looking at the kitchen door like he was hoping Willie Mae'd come out and call us all to dinner. Finally, he must of given up because he suddenly got back into the conversation. "That all sounds real good, Ranger, but how can y'all prove it? Did Vida confess?"

"That's right, Norman," Biggie said. "I found out the whole story when I went home with Vida last night. Once we got her calmed down and in bed, I sat with her and, just before she fell asleep, she told me the whole story. It seems Monk had sweet-talked Itha into going away with him as soon as they found the money."

"I don't believe that," Miss Lonie said. "Why, he abuthed her!"

"My Lord, Lonie," Miss Mattie said. "Don't you ever watch Oprah? Some women like that."

"Well, I wouldn't," Miss Julia said. "I'd take an ax handle after him if he tried to abuse me."

"So, anyway," Biggie said. "Vida took a notion to go over to Monk's house to talk to him. She said she thought she could make him see that it wouldn't be right to uproot De-Wayne right in the middle of the school year. Of course Monk just laughed at her."

"Huh," Mr. Thripp said. "A man's never even sent his kid

so much as a birthday card isn't going to be worrying about his schooling."

"Right," Biggie said, "but remember, we're dealing with a woman who can't tell cow poop from cornbread. It was the only argument she could think of to use on Monk. Anyway, after a while Monk got tired of talking and told her to go on home, but Vida wasn't giving up. Finally, Monk picked up that iron soldier and started toward her."

"The one I found," I said.

"Right," Biggie said. "Well, Vida said he tripped on the carpet and fell down at her feet. That was when Vida got an idea. She remembered how she'd held Cooter down that day on the courthouse lawn. What she did was she just sat on Monk and kept right on talking to him, trying to convince him to leave Itha and DeWayne alone. Vida said he struggled at first then got still. She figured he was listening to reason until she noticed his hand. It had turned white as a sheet. When she turned and looked at his face, it was almost black and his eyes were wide open and staring. Vida just got off of him and went home. She never told a soul about it."

"So will she go to prison?" Mr. Thripp asked.

"Truth is," the ranger said, "we only have her word for it, but if she's telling the truth, Monk's death was an accident. All in all, considering her mental state, I expect her to end up in the state hospital for, probably, the rest of her life."

"Well, if you ask me," Miss Julia said, "I know you shouldn't speak ill of the dead, but I blame Itha. If it wasn't for all that money, I bet she wouldn't have given Monk the time of day."

"Speaking of the money," the ranger said, pulling an envelope out of his pocket, "Here it is, Miss Biggie. Nobody claimed it, so I reckon your museum gets it after all."

"I'm hungry," Monica said.

Just then, Willie Mae flung open the doors to the dining room, letting the smells of roast and gravy and hot rolls and sweet potato pie come floating out.

"Y'all come on and eat," she said.

Willie Mae's Hangtown Fry

Start out with a pint of fresh oysters, small ones, if you can get them. If they give you those big ones, just cut them in two. Now, roll them oysters in a little flour and fry in melted butter that's just starting to sizzle in the pan.

While the oysters are cooking, beat you up a dozen eggs with a little whipping cream or half-and-half. Add in some salt and pepper.

When the oysters are nice and golden brown, pour in the eggs and scramble them all up together. Be careful, though. Stir easy. You don't want to break up your oysters.

When the eggs are soft-scrambled, pour it up on a nice platter and sprinkle the top with crumbled crisp bacon. Stick a little parsley around the edges, and you've got yourself a mighty good dish for brunch or supper.

I generally serve them up with sliced tomatoes from the garden sprinkled with salt and lemon-pepper and drizzled with a little olive oil.

Hot homemade biscuits on the side.